THE SECRET OF CRYBABY HOLLOW

an Abbie, Girl Spy Mystery

by Darren J. Butler

OnStage Publishing, Inc.
Copyright 2002

Abbie, Girl Spy
THE SECRET OF CRYBABY HOLLOW

Published by OnStage Books & Publishing
214 E. Moulton Street N.E.
Decatur, Alabama 35601
256.308.2300 * 888.420.8879

Visit us on the web at **www.abbiegirlspy.com**!

0-9700752-9-4 Hardcover
Printed in the United States of America
November 2002 First Edition

for
Chelsea, Blake, London & Sarah

*   *   *   *   *   *

and for the "group" that started it all
Meredith, Jennifer, Anna, Sarah, Emily & Bekah

*

and my first fan
Lacy

*   *

Special Thanks
Dianne & Margaret

Chapter One

"Okay, Tyler!" Abbie Walker shouted. "This is not funny!" She stopped walking, held her breath and hoped for a response. Abbie sighed and slowly turned around carefully looking into the dense forest. She held her breath again, hoping to hear something that would pinpoint Tyler's hiding place. A whip-poorwill sang in the forest and its song echoed through the woods. She could hear the water in the creek, but there were no sounds that indicated Tyler Graham was anywhere nearby.

"Come on you little punk!" Abbie yelled. She paused, listening to her voice echo in the distance. "If you think you're gonna scare me... you're wrong!"

Abbie listened. Again, there was no response from Tyler. She unzipped her windbreaker, took it off and tied the arms of it around her waist. She whispered to herself, "Come on, Tyler. Don't do this to me."

Abbie walked closer to the rendezvous point where Tyler should have been half an hour ago. Her mind raced with different scenarios of what could have happened. Maybe he was lost. Maybe he was playing a prank on her and hiding behind a tree. What if he had fallen? Maybe he was lying injured in a ditch somewhere...no, not a possibility. Tyler Graham was very athletic. He played first string on the junior high football team. He ran track. He played baseball. There was no way he would be clumsy enough to fall in the woods and hurt himself. Maybe he had just lost track of time.

Abbie took a small notebook from the pocket of her wind-breaker and sat beneath the branches of a large oak tree. As she flipped through the pages of the notebook, Abbie turned and caught a glance of the initials carved in the tree. Dozens of initials, all in individual hearts, covered the "kissing tree." For many, many years, teenagers and adults had carved their initials into the trunk of the old tree. An hour ago Abbie might have considered carving hers and Tyler's initials in this tree, but right now she felt like punching him in the nose.

As she sat beneath the tree contemplating what she should do next, Abbie thought back to her first encounter with Tyler Graham. It had happened on the first day of school in September. What a nerve racking day that was! Abbie felt like her first day in the sixth grade at Albany Junior High had been one small catastrophe after another. She had trouble getting her locker open. She had gotten lost trying to find her second period class. She had been placed in classes with very few familiar faces due to the fact that four elementary schools in town feed into one school for junior high. By third period, she had been totally miserable and ready to call it quits and go home.

Then, it happened. The cutest boy she had ever seen in her whole entire life walked past her in the hall. She had been so taken with him, that she dropped a pile of books to the floor. Lots of kids in the hall stopped to stare or make giggly remarks about her clumsiness. Abbie had quickly come to her senses and stooped down to pick up the scattered mess. Before she realized it, the boy she had been admiring was helping her.

Embarrassed, Abbie had offered a polite, "Thanks," and the boy responded with, "Don't mention it." Abbie had blushed. The boy introduced himself. "I'm Tyler Graham. I just moved here from Florida."

"Really," Abbie had said, trying to ignore the blush she felt on her face.

"Yeah, maybe we'll have some classes together," he'd added.

"Maybe," Abbie had replied.

"See ya round." With those words, Tyler Graham had disappeared into the crowd, leaving a totally smitten Abbie standing still in a hallway of kids scurrying to find their way to their next class. As it turned out, they did end up having one class together - Language Arts with Mrs. Barker. Tyler

Graham had taken the seat next to her, which had made it very hard for Abbie to concentrate.

Of course, in the weeks that followed her feelings for Tyler Graham went up and down like a seesaw. It didn't take Abbie long to notice that Tyler flirted a lot. He loved to flash his pearly white smile and show off his big blue eyes to every girl he found attractive. She wanted Tyler to like her and just her. But, these were new feelings for Abbie. Until Tyler Graham showed up, she really had not been that interested in boys, unlike her friend Sarah Martin who had been chasing boys on the playground since kindergarten.

Abbie almost died when Mrs. Barker paired Tyler with her for this assignment. She had hoped to be paired with Amy or Renee. Even Kirk would have been better help than Tyler. She knew how this assignment would go. She would end up doing all of the work and Tyler would charm his way out of any kind of responsibility and take half the credit for all of Abbie's work.

The assignment was simple. Pick one of Albany's urban legends that Mrs. Barker had listed on the board, and make a video presentation using interviews and video of the subject. Abbie had let Tyler make the choice. He had chosen the legendary spooky story of Crybaby Hollow. The hollow was located at the edge of town right smack in the middle of a very thick forest. Only a one-lane dirt road cut through it, unless someone wanted to count the creek that was an overspill of the Tennessee River. Over the creek was an old wooden bridge and according to the legend, if a person stood on the bridge at night and placed a candy bar on the railing of the bridge, he would hear a baby cry.

Abbie and Tyler had interviewed four people and got four completely different stories of "why" they could hear a baby cry. This afternoon was the time to get footage of the hollow and the bridge. Tyler operated the camera and Abbie did all of the narration. After they had wrapped up the closing statement, Abbie suggested that they separate and go ten minutes in opposite directions. She thought they might find something interesting to add to the final shot of the presentation. They decided to meet at the kissing tree twenty minutes later.

Abbie looked down at her watch. It was almost six o'clock and Tyler was now forty-five minutes late. She was already late for supper and would be in big trouble with her mother. "This is great, just great," Abbie said out loud. "I can't believe I'm out here in the middle of the woods waiting on him!"

Abbie kicked a stone and some dirt in frustration. "Now what? Becca, if you could see me now you would be laughing your head off! I'm out here with the cutest guy in school... at the kissing tree with nobody to kiss!" The thought of Becca made her sad. She missed her best friend and would give anything in the world for her to be here right now. Becca had moved to Memphis over four months ago and it had been a hard adjustment for Abbie.

"Okay Kirk, I know what you would do," she reasoned, pretending that her friends were standing there in front of her. "You would walk back to town and let Tyler sit out here and rot." Abbie paced back and forth thinking out loud. "Sarah, on the other hand, you would be carving yours and Tyler's initials into the kissing tree. Becca...Becca, what would you do?" It didn't take Abbie long to come up with a solution to this question. "The same thing I would do. Go find the little punk!"

Abbie got up and brushed off her jacket and jeans. She strolled down the dirt road to the wooden bridge and climbed onto the lower railing of to see if she could see any sign of Tyler. The only thing she saw was the creek and the trees and the birds. But, this was not stopping her. Tyler went that way and so was she!

She stepped down from the railing and walked towards the end of the bridge. As she neared the end of the bridge, her pace slowed and then she stopped, though unsure of why. Abbie suddenly had a feeling of deja-vu. She looked over her shoulder towards the other end of the bridge. A startling image of bright headlights in the dark flashed in her mind. Abbie felt a cold shiver race over her and goose bumps rose on her arms.

For almost three years, Abbie had experienced a recurring dream of being chased on her bicycle. Every now and then, something triggered fragmented memories of the dream, but Abbie had never been able to remember the whole thing.

Abbie slowly stepped backwards onto the dirt road. Something about this bridge and the dirt road were strangely familiar, but she couldn't quite put her finger on it. As far as she knew she had only been to Crybaby Hollow once before and that was two weeks ago after she and Tyler received the assignment. Her dad had driven down the road and showed her the bridge, but it had been broad daylight.

Abbie shook off the eerie feeling and walked down to the creek. The water in the creek had risen over the past two weeks with all of the rain. Sparkles of sunlight danced across the water as it flowed gently over the rocks that filled the creek.

Abbie followed the creek as it wound its way through the woods like a snake. The more she walked, the creepier she felt. It was almost dark and the last place she wanted to be was alone in the woods at night. She stepped on a large flat rock and stopped to look around. Something in the distance caught her eye. It was a candy bar wrapper. Tyler had been eating a chocolate candy bar when they separated. Was it his?

Abbie reached for the wrapper. She knew it was Tyler's the second she picked it up. The cheerleaders were selling this kind of candy bar to raise money and Tyler had bought one from Heidi Cook after school. "So, he did come this way," she thought to herself. She wadded up the wrapper and shoved it into her pocket. "Litterbug," she said to herself.

Cautiously stepping from one rock to another in the creek bed, Abbie proceeded further into the woods. As she rounded the bend of the creek, Abbie caught a glimpse of Tyler's bright red jacket about fifty feet ahead. He sat on the ground studying something, but Abbie couldn't see what it was. Okay, buster, I'm gonna get you. I'll sneak up behind you and scare you to death.

Abbie took her time and carefully moved towards Tyler. One wrong step and he would know that she was sneaking up behind him. She got as close as she dared, counted to three in her head, and sprang at him yelling as loudly as she could. Startled, Tyler quickly scooted away from the pouncing Abbie. When she landed on the spot where Tyler had sat, she came face to face with the object he had been studying so intently.

Lying in the water was a skull. Unfortunately, Abbie recognized that it wasn't the skull of a dog or cow or other wild animal. It was a human skull and it definitely didn't belong in the creek at Crybaby Hollow.

Chapter Two

October 29th

It's never a good sign when you arrive home in a police car...even if a friend of the family is driving. This afternoon, Tyler and I found a human skull in the creek at Crybaby Hollow. I tried my very best not to be Nancy Drew, but I just couldn't help myself. I mean, it's a human skull and that's just not something you find every day. So, we used Tyler's cell phone to call my friend, Sergeant Jane Galloway. She and her partner met us out in the woods and they took some pictures and bagged up the skull. When she offered to bring me home I didn't dare refuse. I knew I was going to be in deep trouble with Mom, so I thought maybe Jane could smooth *things out.*

Didn't work. In front of Jane, Mom was thankful and excited to see me, but when the door closed...well, there was silence. I think some people call it the "calm before the storm." I am now up in my room waiting for Mother Tornado to blow through and tear me to pieces.

Abbie closed her journal and laid it on the bed. She crept over to her bedroom door and listened. She couldn't hear anything downstairs. Her mother was probably cooking supper and hopefully cooling down a bit. Abbie carefully cracked the door open just enough to peer down the hall. The hallway was dark, but the aroma of the standard Tuesday night meatloaf hit her in the face.

Abbie sat down on her bed and fluffed the pillows behind her against the headboard. She picked up her journal and flipped back to read some earlier entries.

September 3rd

I can't believe it's finally here! Junior High! Tomorrow, I will officially be a sixth grade student at Albany Junior High. Tonight, I picked out my clothes for tomorrow and hung them on my closet door. I've written my name on all of my notebooks and packed my backpack.

Oh, and you won't believe what I found this afternoon when I got back from the pool. Apparently, while I was at the pool swimming, my mother took it upon herself to do a little shopping. She bought me socks and some new shirts and...hidden on the bottom of the pile were three training bras and one of those with padding! Is this some kind of joke? Does she really expect me to wear these? Oh, and no conversation... not a word. I thought this might be the beginning of one of those little talks that she starts and Dad finishes, but no...not one word. I am assuming that since we have to dress out for PE, she thinks I want one and am too embarrassed to ask. I am not embarrassed. I just don't want one...at least not until I have to. I have placed these things at the bottom of my top drawer. For the time being I will continue to wear my undershirt. I know that a lot of girls my age, like Sarah, look forward to all this stuff, but I guess I'm just not ready. I mean shaving my legs is bad enough, do I have to add anything else to my misery?

I have made a decision. I am going to put the detective business on the back burner for a while. After the summer I've had, I think I need to take a break and concentrate on junior high. I feel guilty in a way...like I'm letting Becca down, but you know, she's not here and she's got new friends and well...I just want to fit in at school. I'm scared that kids will call me Nancy Drew or worse, Jessica Fletcher, behind my back and make fun of me. So, for now, the secret underground office will have to stay locked up.

I am going to try and go to sleep, although I'm much too excited. Maybe I should read? I have just started re-reading the Harry Potter series. I think I'll read one chapter and hit the hay.

Abbie looked up from her journal. Any minute now, she expected the door to open and someone to enter. Hopefully, it would be her dad, who would be there to make peace between Abbie and her mother. If it was her mother, she would bite her bottom lip, control her tongue and only reply with "yes, ma'am" or "no, ma'am." Anything else might result in being grounded. With Halloween in a couple of days, she couldn't risk it. To get her mind off her impending doom, she picked up her journal again.

September 4th

I never thought I would say this, but I think I'm in love. The day started out bad and got even worse, but to top it all off, I was checking out this guy and

I dropped all of my stuff on the floor in front of everyone. All these kids were staring at me and then the really cute guy I was checking out came to my rescue. His name is Tyler Graham and he just moved here from Cocoa Beach, Florida, and...

Abbie slammed her journal shut. "I can't believe I wrote that!" she said to herself. She wanted to take the pages and rip them out...but she didn't. She clutched her journal to her and buried her head in her pillow as she remembered that day.

Abbie had definitely been bitten by the love bug. After writing in her journal that afternoon, she had cranked up her stereo, and had started doing all kinds of things that were totally out of character for her. She had tried on all kinds of clothes trying to find just the right outfit for the next day. She put on a pair of earrings to show off her newly pierced ears. She dug through her drawers for the make-up that her crazy Aunt Laurie had bought for her. And to top off that afternoon of craziness, she had tried on the padded bra to see if it would make her look more grown-up for Tyler Graham.

Abbie grumbled to herself at the memory of what she had done that afternoon. Then, the final image flashed in her head. In the mirror she had seen herself all dolled up and that's when common sense hit her over the head. She told her reflection, "Mirror, mirror on the wall, you are

Sarah Martin, after all."

Abbie giggled to herself. Now, it was funny. Thank God, no one had seen her dressed like that. What if her mother had walked in...or her dad? Or, even worse, what if Sarah had seen her? Abbie tossed her journal on the bed and rolled over to look up at the ceiling. "Thank God for small favors," she repeated to herself.

Then, it happened. What she had been waiting for came walking in the door. Her mother had entered the room. To Abbie's surprise, there were no shouts, no tears, no ranting and raving...nothing.

"Supper will be ready in about fifteen minutes. Your dad should be home by then. Have you started your homework?" her mother asked in a calm voice.

"Uh...I just have to read a chapter in science and then I'll be done," Abbie replied.

"Good," her mother started out of the room and then came back to stand in the doorway.

Uh, oh. Here it comes. Abbie thought to herself.

"Now that you're in junior high, your dad and I know that you are going to be out with friends and you'll want to go places and...hang-out with them," her mother began, "but if you're going to be late...just call us. We just want to know where you are, okay?"

Abbie nodded and smiled. "Sure, mom. I will. I'm sorry I was late. It won't happen again."

"Yes it will," her mother laughed as she pulled Abbie's door shut behind her.

Something miraculous had just occurred. No lecture. No punishment. Abbie was off the hook with her mother's version of a warning. Abbie fell back onto her bed and kicked her feet in the air. She picked up her journal and added to her last entry:

Just when you think you have your parents fig-ured out, they go and surprise you. Something else happened today on the bridge at Crybaby Hollow. I was standing at one end of the bridge with the feel-ing that I had been there before. It was very weird and I think it may have something to do with the dreams I've been having. Maybe they're all con-nected somehow.

*   *   *

At supper, Abbie gave her mom and dad the full story of what happened in the woods that afternoon. After the part about the skull, her dad chuckled.

"Abbie, I'm afraid that someone was just playing a prank on you," her dad explained. "Crybaby Hollow is one of those places that kids use for scaring people. In fact, when I was a freshman in high school, the seniors took us out to the bridge and dumped us at eleven o'clock one night. Then, we had to walk back to the main road in the dark."

"That doesn't sound too bad," Abbie said.

"No, not bad at all, until they drove away and we started hearing things out in the woods. We walked down the road and it got darker and darker because the trees blocked the moonlight and then all of a sudden, right in front of us, a car's headlights flashed and the engine started revving up and we started running in the opposite direction."

"What happened?" Abbie asked excitedly.

"We ran as fast as we could and then we heard a bunch of seniors laughing their heads off 'cause they scared us," her father explained.

Abbie giggled at the thought of her teenage dad running from a bunch of older kids. Even her mother was laughing. "So, you think that skull is just a Halloween joke?"

Her dad smiled back at her. "Yeah, honey. Someone's just pulling your leg. I wouldn't give it another thought."

Abbie didn't give it another thought. Her dad was right. She probably should have never called the cops. She should have picked it up and brought it home to use in their presentation. Maybe they would have gotten extra points.

Chapter Three

Heidi Cook stopped the VCR and turned off the television. "So anyway, my dad says that people that live near the river have actually dug up their yards looking for the lost gold shipment. Can you believe it? I mean, like who would do something...like so totally bizarre?" The students in Abbie's class giggled.

"Thank you, Heidi," Mrs. Barker said. She started clapping and the rest of the class joined her. "That's one of our most famous urban legends. It's hard to believe that that much gold could just vanish into thin air." She stopped, leaving the mystery of the missing treasure lingering for everyone to contemplate. Mrs. Barker referred back to her notebook and looked towards Abbie. "Miss Walker, are you ready?"

"Yes ma'am," Abbie replied and got out of her seat. Tyler Graham was not present for the big day. He was at the dentist, but Abbie didn't care. The presentation would go much smoother without him.

Chapter Three

Abbie put the videotape into the VCR and flipped on the television. "Tyler and I call our project, 'The Secret of Crybaby Hollow.' On the video you are about to watch, you'll see four interviews with people who live in Albany. Each of them had a story to tell us about the mysterious baby's cry. We hope you enjoy it."

Abbie pressed the play button and sat down in a chair near the front of the class. She watched the expressions of her classmates as they watched the tape. When it finished she turned off the tape and television and addressed the class for her final statement. "As you can see, just like all urban legends, everyone's got a different story to tell about 'why' you can hear a baby's cry at the bridge."

Just as Abbie was finishing, a girl in the back of the room raised her hand. It was Ginny McAbee. "Abbie, did you try it? Did you hear the baby cry?"

"Uh, well, no, actually. Tyler said he and his friends went out there one night and tried it, but he said he didn't hear anything but the crickets," Abbie joked as the rest of the class laughed with her.

Mrs. Barker rose from her seat and flipped on the lights. "Well, that concludes our video presentations for today. We'll view more projects tomorrow."

Billy Miller's hand shot into the air. "Mrs. Barker, I want to ask Abbie something."

Worried about "what" Billy Miller would ask, Mrs. Barker hesitated for a moment. "Is it really important?"

Billy nodded and Mrs. Barker allowed him to speak. "I just want to know where the skull fits into the picture?"

A few students sniggered, but the rest of the class turned their heads in unison towards Abbie, eagerly waiting for her response.

Abbie froze. She knew this was bound to happen. "There's really not much to tell. Tyler and I were looking for an interesting shot to add to the end of our video, and we separated. We agreed to meet back at..." Abbie hesitated. She didn't dare mention the word "kissing tree" in front of these clowns. "The bridge. When Tyler didn't come back I went looking for him. He found the skull a good ways down the creek. We used his mom's cell phone to call the police and they came and took some pictures and bagged it up and took it away. That's about it."

Over half the class put their hands in the air to ask a question. Even Sarah had her hand up, but Abbie decided to call on Renee Swanson.

"So, what did the cops say? Who did the skull belong to?" Renee asked.

"Well, the police really don't know, but from the look of the skull, it was pretty old, at least that's what they said," Abbie explained.

"Is that what you think?" asked Heidi Cook, who was seated right in front of Abbie on the front row.

Abbie felt very uncomfortable. She was trying hard to blend in with the rest of the kids and not come across as a "private eye." This is exactly what she had tried to avoid. Kirk stared at her, not understanding why she was stammering. "W-well," she began nervously, "My dad and I were talking about this last night and he thinks...and I agree with him, that it's just someone's idea of a practical joke. I-I mean, Halloween is in a couple of days and a lot of teenagers hang out there and...well, I'm sure it's just a prank."

Billy Miller spoke out, "But where would they get a skull?"

"Anywhere, really. It could have come from one of those science supply companies or uh...well, you know." Abbie caught herself before she sounded like a detective again. The bell rang. "Saved by the bell," she thought to herself. Abbie quickly went to her desk, gathered up her stuff and made a beeline for the door to avoid further interrogation. She was the first student out of the room. Kirk and Sarah, who were trying to catch up with her, got stuck in the crowd of students trying to exit the classroom. They finally caught up with Abbie at her locker.

She was kneeling on the floor trying to make the combination lock work. Kirk and Sarah approached her and stood there watching her as she tried unsuccessfully to open the locker.

Kirk finally broke the silence. "What was that all about?"

"What was what about?" Abbie continued to give her attention to her combination lock.

"You were all weird in there. You acted like you were afraid to tell them what you think happened." Kirk waited for a response from Abbie but she ignored him.

He stood there glaring at her, waiting for an answer. An obese boy named, Ralph Hillard, approached them, and started fiddling with his locker, which was right above Abbie's.

Abbie finally got her locker open and put her stuff

inside. She glanced up to Kirk who was still waiting for an answer. She lowered her voice and said, "That's because I don't know what really happened with that skull. We just found it...okay? There was no blood, no guts, no fingerprints, no–" Abbie was cut off by a shower of books and papers falling on her head. Sarah and Kirk jumped back and Abbie stood up to Ralph Hillard.

"Oops," he said without one bit of concern.

Abbie stared him down and said, "Look, Ralph. Can't you clean out that pigsty so your junk doesn't fall on me every time you open your locker?"

Ralph, who looked like he could care less, chuckled and ignored her as he poked around in his locker. Abbie pushed Ralph's stuff out of her way and joined Kirk and Sarah who were laughing. "Laugh a little louder. Maybe you can humiliate me some more!" she exclaimed.

"Well, it was funny," Sarah smirked.

"Yeah, the first couple of times, maybe, but when it happens three for four times a week for two months, it's not so funny anymore, believe me!" Abbie explained as she rubbed the sore spot on her head.

Kirk, who had his laughter under control, asked, "Abbie, what was the deal back there in class?

Abbie turned and slowly started walking down the hall. Kirk and Sarah followed on either side. "I don't know," she began. Abbie was directing this conversation to Kirk, since he was part of AGS Investigations and Sarah wasn't. "I guess I'm scared that the other kids will make fun of me... well, us, if they find out about...you know."

"The detective agency?" Sarah asked as if it was public knowledge.

Abbie stopped. She glared at Sarah and gave her a polite little smile. She grabbed Kirk by the arm and pushed him over to the side of the hall.

"Ouch! That hurts! Let go!" Kirk protested.

"You told her?"

"Uh...well, it's not like she didn't already know. You and Becca have been at this for almost three years. I just mentioned to her that–"

Abbie put her hand up to his mouth to shut him up. "Blabbermouth." Furious with him, she started walking again, alone.

"Hey, Abbie!" Sarah called out. Abbie stopped and allowed Sarah to catch up with her. "I'm not going to tell anyone what Kirk told me, so you don't have to worry."

"Thank you," Abbie replied politely. Kirk had rejoined them, but he was staying at arm's length from Abbie. They all started walking down the hall together, but they didn't say another word. Abbie and Sarah had PE next and Kirk had history, so they parted at the end of the hall.

Abbie and Sarah made their way through the crowd of students to the girls' locker room downstairs. Sarah knew that Abbie was a little ticked off, so she decided to go straight to her locker and leave Abbie alone for now.

As Sarah pulled her Albany Junior High t-shirt over her head, she was bombed with washcloths of all different shapes, sizes and colors. The locker room roared with laughter. Sarah jerked a white washcloth from her head and waved it in the air for everyone to see. She looked around the locker room, for the culprits, but they were hiding from her.

"Very cute! Oh, this is very original, girls! How long did it take you to think this one up? Huh? That pool thing was four, count them ladies, four months ago! Hey, do any of you want to borrow some of these? You sure could use them!"

Laughter continued as Sarah threw the washcloth to the floor with the others. She looked over to see Abbie on the floor holding her stomach from laughing so hard. Sarah walked over to her, crossed her arms and started tapping her foot. She waited for Abbie to stop, but Abbie kept laughing. When she looked up at Sarah and tried to speak, she just started laughing all over again, uncontrollably.

Sarah cracked a sarcastic grin and said, "Good! Glad you can laugh at my expense." Sarah decided to sit down on the bench beside the lockers until Abbie got control of herself.

The pool incident had happened in June. Sarah had stuffed a couple of washcloths into her older sister's bikini top and dived off the diving board at the community pool. Sarah went down to the bottom, but her top and the washcloths stayed on the surface. Abbie had jumped in with her towel and saved Sarah from total humiliation.

Coach Johnson blew her whistle and yelled into the locker room for the slowpokes to hurry up. Abbie's laughing slowed and she sat up on the floor in front of Sarah. "I'm sorry," she began. "If you could have seen the look on your face when those washcloths were falling all over you..."

Chapter Three

Sarah could see now that Abbie had tears streaming down her cheeks from all the laughter.

Sarah thought Abbie was going to start laughing all over again, but she didn't. Instead, Abbie tried to apologize again, but Sarah just shook her head, trying not to burst out into laughter herself. "Did you know about this?"

"No," Abbie insisted. "I swear. I knew nothing about it." Abbie took her t-shirt and wiped the tears from her face.

"This is so humiliating. I mean, I make one little 'stuffing' mistake and it's going to haunt me for the rest of my life!" Sarah exclaimed. " I can see it now. I'll be fifty years old and walking down the street and someone will still be bringing it up."

"Well, if no one does, I'm sure not going to let you forget it," Abbie assured her.

"It's not like they have anything to brag about either. It's like training bra city down here," Sarah said sarcastically. "Except for you and your undershirts!"

"Okay, okay, go ahead and poke fun at me and my flatness, but you're not going to get me into one of those things until I have to," Abbie protested.

"You would have loved the seventies. My mom says–" Coach Johnson's whistle blew again and Abbie got up from the floor and quickly put on her tennis shoes.

"Well, I'd rather be like this than be like Lizzie," Abbie pointed out.

"For real! It's a wonder she doesn't fall over on her face from being so top heavy," Sarah joked.

"I wonder if she has back aches from having to hold

all of that up?" Abbie asked in a serious tone and then looked at Sarah. Both girls exploded in laughter once again. "We've got to stop this, my side is starting to hurt from laughing so hard."

"Hey, you know a friend of mine told me once to just be myself and stop trying to be something I'm not," Sarah said.

Abbie closed the door to her locker and looked back to Sarah. "So, I should just listen to my own advice, huh?" Abbie asked as she wiped her eyes again.

"Yep, pretty much. So what if you have your own detective agency? Someday you'll be working for the FBI while the rest of them are working for the PTA!"

Abbie gave Sarah a high five and said, "Thanks."

"Don't mention it," Sarah replied. The girls started walking for the steps that led up to the gym. "Don't be worried about the kids laughing at you because of the things you and Becca have done. Remember when your picture was in the paper after you came back from Memphis this summer?"

"How could I forget it?" Abbie replied. "The head-line said, 'Local Girl Finds Missing Ducks and Diamonds'."

"Yeah, well, no one was laughing about that," Sarah assured her. "Everyone I know thought it was real cool."

"Really?"

"Really," Sarah promised. There was a slight lull in the conversation as they walked up the steps. When they got to the top, they discovered that the girls in their PE class were running laps around the gym. Sarah and Abbie joined them, trying not to look too tardy.

"So, are you and Kirk on a case right now?" Sarah asked as they jogged.

"No," Abbie admitted. "I've really not thought about any of that stuff with school getting started and all."

"Yeah, I know what you mean."

"But, Heidi Cook's project on that lost gold shipment sounds very interesting," Abbie suggested.

Sarah thought about this for a few seconds before responding. "But doesn't that skull make you curious? Don't want to know who it belonged to?"

"I told you, it was somebody's idea of a joke," Abbie reminded her.

"And you were serious about that?"

"Yeah, I think my dad's right. Just a joke, nothing more," Abbie was done with this subject. If she heard one more word about it, she was going to explode.

"So, what's next?" Sarah asked, almost out of breath.

"I think I'm gonna go over to the Old State Bank this afternoon after school," Abbie answered.

"Can I join you?" Sarah asked.

"Sure," Abbie gave in. "We'll meet at the bike rack after school, okay?"

"Great!" Sarah said excitedly. The whistle blew and the girls stopped their running. "Oh, but you might not want to tell Becca you're letting me tag along. She doesn't like me."

"That's Becca's problem," replied Abbie. "She has new friends...and so do I."

Chapter Four

What was Kirk Simpson thinking? Abbie was well aware that Sarah knew about AGS Investigations, but she had tried to keep it low-key around her, considering Sarah's previous actions. Just four months ago, she and Abbie were practically at each other's throats following the "pool incident."

Following Sarah's topless plunge into the community pool, Abbie had taken her into the locker room until the kids around the pool left. Abbie could remember how furious she was at Sarah for lashing out at her, but Abbie had given her a good taste of her own medicine. The scene was crystal clear in her head:

"Okay, I'm just going to say it and get it off my chest, so to speak. Are you crazy?"

Sarah looked at her and for probably the first time in her life was speechless and waited for what Abbie was going to say next.

Mocking Sarah, Abbie started in on her. "I should

have never dived off the platform wearing a bikini!" Abbie repeated Sarah's words back to her like a machine gun. "You should have never stuffed yourself to make yourself look like you're sixteen years old. When are you going to get it through your thick head that you're eleven and eleven year old girls shouldn't be trying to get boys, especially older boys, to notice them because of how grown up they look!"

"Well excuse me if I don't want to play with dolls and have tea parties," Sarah said trying to defend herself against this accusation.

"Sarah! In case you didn't notice, nobody else was running to help you out there. They were laughing, Sarah, and they were laughing loudly! Heaven only knows why I jumped in after you like that. I should have let you find your own way out the pool and let you make a complete fool out of yourself!" Abbie's temper had flared so much that her face had turned red. She turned away from Sarah and headed for the door.

"Well," Sarah replied in a smart tone. "At least I'm not running around the city pretending to be a detective. Who's trying to pretend to be grown-up now? Oh, I almost forgot, you're little friend Becca has left you so I guess the dynamic duo is all finished. Guess you'll have to pull your dolls back out of the closet and put away your finger print kit for a few years, huh?"

At first, Abbie thought about turning on Sarah and beating the daylights out of her, but she knew that wouldn't solve anything. She slowly let the door close once again. Abbie stared Sarah straight in the eye and walked over to her. Sarah probably thought she was about to get beat up, but Abbie remained calm and stopped only inches from her. "You know, I feel sorry for you. I've tried to be your friend but the problem is, you don't know how to be a friend to anyone. I've taken up for you, I've helped you and today I saved your butt out there. And, then when I try to give you a little good advice you turn things around and make fun of me and my friends. The sad thing is that I still want to be your friend and that's the only reason I don't take my t-shirt back right now! That either makes me a fairly decent person or really stupid now doesn't it?"

In the days following that fateful event, Sarah had come and apologized for what she had said. It was at that moment that Abbie saw Sarah in a different light. Abbie, Becca, Sarah and Kirk had been in the same class since kindergarten. Even when they were little, Sarah was always the bossy, selfish type as well as being a total airhead. However, she and Becca had always been nice to her. They had invited her to all of their birthday parties and spend the night parties, but it was only out of politeness and the encouragement of their mothers.

Abbie was beginning to notice a change in Sarah. She was still an airhead and still a little bossy, but much more tolerable. With Becca gone, Sarah was becoming one of her closest friends. However, there were still things about AGS Investigations that Sarah didn't know and Abbie wasn't sure she wanted to tell her. If Kirk had told Sarah about the secret underground office, then she would just have to beat him to a pulp.

Chapter Four

School let out at three o'clock and Abbie met Kirk and Sarah by the bike rack. Kirk was already there, unlocking his bicycle and fastening his backpack to his bike. As Abbie approached him, he glanced up but didn't say anything. She had given him the silent treatment for the rest of the school day, but now it was time to forgive and forget get back to work.

"Hey, Kirk," Abbie began.

"Hey," Kirk responded timidly.

"Sarah and I are going to the Old State Bank to do some research on the lost gold shipment," Abbie explained.

"Oh, Heidi's report. Yes, that was very interesting. Do you think it's still out there somewhere?" Kirk asked. The tension between them had lifted and things were obviously back to normal.

"Yeah, I do," said Abbie. "It has to be out there somewhere."

Sarah, who desperately wanted to be included, jumped into the conversation. "But people have been... like looking for it for a really long time. Don't you think someone would have found it by now?"

"Maybe they're just not looking in the right place," Abbie suggested as she unlocked her bike.

"True. It's worth a go, don't you think?" Kirk aimed this question at Sarah.

"Yeah, sure," Sarah replied instantly. "I mean if we found it, I could buy like hundreds of pairs of shoes..." Sarah noticed that Kirk gave Abbie a look of amazement at her inclusion.

Kirk stammered, worried that it was his fault that

Sarah wanted to be involved in the investigation.
"Uh...well, Sarah..."

Abbie interrupted, "Yeah, you could buy out the shoe department in the mall!"

Kirk's look of surprise was priceless. Had his ears deceived him? Was Abbie really considering letting Sarah in on a potential case? The girls were laughing at the thought of all those shoes, so he played along and laughed with them.

"Of course, you'll have all those shoes and nothing to wear with them," he joked.

Sarah shot him a look that told him she didn't appreciate his sly remarks about her shopping habits. Abbie came to his rescue.

"Okay, well, we're going to the Old State Bank. Kirk, why don't you go over to the library and search the microfiche for any news articles about the lost gold shipment. Maybe you'll turn up some clues there."

Kirk, who was very thankful that Abbie had saved him from Sarah, responded with an "okay" and mounted his bike. As he quickly rode away from them, he called back, "I'll check in with you later!"

Sarah glared at him as he rode off the school grounds. "He forgets that I'm armed," Sarah said smugly.

Abbie, who had also been watching Kirk ride away, turned back to Sarah in disbelief at this remark. "What? What do you mean you're armed?"

Sarah held her fingers up in the air. "Well-filed claws."

The girls burst out into laughter as they mounted their bikes. It would take them twenty-minutes to get there by bicycle and Abbie was a little afraid that Sarah might start whining halfway there, but she didn't. When they crossed over the main street that ran through Albany, Abbie motioned for Sarah to follow her so she could stop at Mr. Ed's grocery store for a small snack.

Mr. Ed's store was a small corner grocery that had been there for years and years. As the girls entered the store, the little bell above the door jingled and Abbie caught a glimpse of Mr. Ed looking up from the meat counter.

Good old Mr. Ed was as chipper as usual. Abbie noticed that he was moving a bit slower these days. However, Mr. Ed always perked up when Abbie came around.

Sarah was surveying the store with curiosity. The shelves were packed with canned goods and other grocery items. But the thing that caught Sarah's eye was the large assortment of candy that Mr. Ed stocked.

"Where have you been young lady?" Mr. Ed asked as he walked towards them from the back of the store. "I haven't seen hide nor hair of you and your dad in a month of Sundays."

"Well, I've been busy, Mr. Ed and you know how Dad is with work," Abbie responded with a sigh. "Junior High is nothing but homework, test, homework, test, test, test and test!"

"So who do you have here?" Mr. Ed inquired motioning to Sarah.

"This is my friend, Sarah Martin."

"Nice to meet you," Sarah said as she dug through her pockets for change.

Chapter Four

"Are you new around here?" Mr. Ed quizzed as he slid Abbie a pack of M & M's, her usual.

Sarah paused for a second wondering how he knew what Abbie wanted. "Oh no. I've lived here all my life. I guess I've just never been here before," Sarah said, a little embarrassed.

Abbie got two drinks from the old-fashioned cooler in the back corner of the store and brought them to the counter for a bottle opener.

"Coke in a glass bottle. That's cool!" Sarah was intrigued by the little glass bottles of Coke. Mr. Ed looked at her surprised.

"She doesn't get out much," Abbie teased.

"Hey!" Sarah said with a little disgust.

"Just kidding," Abbie apologized. The girls put their money on the counter and popped the tops off their bottled drinks.

While Mr. Ed counted their money and put it in the cash register, Abbie decided to run the gold shipment story by him. After all, he had been very useful on the missing locket case. It was Mr. Ed that had given her the clues about the old house in the middle of the woods.

"Mr. Ed? Do you know anything about a gold shipment that was lost during the Civil War?"

"Of course. Everybody knows about that," he replied casually. Abbie was a little put off. If everyone knew, why didn't she?

"So what's the scoop?" she asked inquisitively.

"As the story goes, there was a shipment of gold

that was being brought down river to the Old State Bank building. Word reached town that the northern troops were headed this way, so they diverted from the original destination and hid the gold somewhere along the river. The northern troops came through, did their damage and after it was all over, there was no one left alive who knew where the gold was."

"Could the northern troops have taken it?" Sarah asked.

"Possibly, but everyone thinks it's buried somewhere around here. I know folks that dug up their backyards cause they thought it was there," Mr. Ed replied with a grin.

"We've heard about that," said Abbie. "A girl in our class did a report about it."

"Got you curious, didn't it young'un?" quizzed Mr. Ed. He knew how much Abbie enjoyed a good mystery.

"Yeah," said Abbie casually. "I think it's worth looking into."

"I hate to disappoint you, but finding that gold is gonna be like finding a needle in a haystack," Mr. Ed laughed, dashing any hope that Abbie had of finding it.

"Well, we hate to run, but the Old Bank's going to close in half an hour," said Abbie as she gave Mr. Ed a hug.

"Don't be a stranger, young lady. And bring your dad around to see me," he said as the girls headed for the door. Abbie and Sarah mounted their bikes and started pedaling down the street towards the Old Bank building.

"This may be a dead end, Sarah," Abbie pointed out.

"Why do you say that?"

"Well, the way I look at it, if this gold has been missing for a hundred and forty years, and no one's found it yet, we're probably not going to have much luck," Abbie explained.

"But it'll be fun looking. Come on!" Sarah pedaled a little faster and Abbie picked up the pace to catch up with her. It didn't take them long to reach the historic Old State Bank building. The building was at least a hundred and sixty years old. Four large columns adorned the front of the building with gigantic concrete slab steps on either side. The fountain outside was off, but the American flag made a whipping sound as it fought the wind.

The Old State Bank building had stopped being a bank years ago and was now a museum. It had been one of four buildings that didn't get burned to the ground by the Yankees during the Civil War. Instead, the northern troops had used the Old State Bank as a headquarters for the Union army.

The girls parked their bikes on the right side of the building and climbed up the steps. They entered the main lobby and looked at the brochures for a moment before a tall, slender gentleman wearing glasses appeared. "May I help you, ladies?"

"Hi, my name is Abbie Walker and this is Sarah Martin. We're doing a project for school about the lost gold shipment during the Civil War. Do you have any information on that?" Abbie had cut right to the point. No use beating around the bush.

The gentleman smiled and mumbled, "Gold chaser," to himself as he walked over to a filing cabinet in the corner. "If I had a nickel for everyone who asked about that I would be a rich man."

Abbie's enthusiasm wilted. She was just another tourist chasing imaginary pots of gold at the end of a non-existent rainbow. "So, a lot of people ask you about it, huh?"

"You could say that. In fact, a girl was in here just the other day. Oh, by the way, I'm Ray Strickland. I'm the curator here at the Old State Bank," he said as he flipped through the files.

"It's nice to meet you," Abbie replied.

Ray searched for a few seconds more and finally pulled out a file from the drawer. "Here it is. I did a paper on the Old Bank when I was in college down at Auburn. All of the known facts about the gold shipment legend are in this paper."

"Thank you," Abbie said as she started glancing through it.

"You know, I looked for it myself, but never found one clue as to where it was hidden," he admitted.

Sarah was trying to look over Abbie's shoulder. "So, you think it's still out there? You don't think the Yankees took it?"

"I don't know. It's a mystery, that's for sure," Ray replied.

Just the words that Abbie wanted to hear. It was her theme song, "It's a mystery, that's for sure."

Abbie decided to read it more thoroughly later. She tucked it under her arm, and looked up at Ray. "Well, thank you for your time. This will help a lot." She shook his hand and Sarah followed like a puppy.

When they reached the steps outside, Abbie took a

seat next to one of the columns and placed Mr. Strickland's report in her backpack. She folded her legs and pulled her knees close to her chin. She rested her arms there. Abbie aimlessly stared towards the traffic on the highway that ran parallel to the Old Bank.

"Is that it? Aren't we going to look for clues or fingerprints or something?" Sarah was a little shocked at how easily Abbie had given up.

"There's something he's not telling us," Abbie replied calmly. Her brow was crinkled and she was in deep thought.

"What do you mean?" Sarah asked, intrigued.

"I don't know. I can't put my finger on it, but there was just something about that whole thing that makes me think he knows something more."

Sarah crinkled her forehead and gave Abbie a look. "You know what I think?"

"What?" Abbie replied, not even looking back at her.

"I think you're paranoid! He told you that he couldn't even find it himself and look at him! He's a history nut. Major geek!" Sarah marched down the steps. "Are you coming?"

Abbie didn't say a word. She was thinking. Her mind searched for answers. Her intuition told her that there was more to Mr. Strickland and his knowledge of the gold. She followed Sarah down the steps. They mounted their bikes and pedaled away.

When Abbie took another direction, Sarah yelled ahead, "Why are you going that way?"

Abbie called back to her, "Let's go downtown and

get a milkshake at the coffeehouse around the corner from the theatre."

Sarah let out a "yes!" and the girls pedaled down the brick-covered historic street until they reached the Princess Theatre. The theatre was originally a horse stable, which had been converted into a vaudeville theatre and then into a movie theater. Now it was the Princess Theatre Center for the Performing Arts. Abbie crossed the street and jumped the curb, so that she could stop at the front of the theatre.

"What'cha doin'?" Sarah asked.

"I want to find out what's coming," Abbie replied as she scanned the display boards in front of the theatre.

Sarah's eye caught it first. "Abbie! Come here, look!" She motioned for Abbie to join her at one of the window displays.

"What?" Abbie asked.

"Your favorite show! They're having auditions for The Secret Garden right after Christmas."

Abbie's eyes widened and her face lit up. "I can't believe it! They're doing The Secret Garden! I love that show!"

"Like everyone in the world knows that!" Sarah replied sarcastically. "You should try out."

"No way," Abbie replied.

"Yes! You should! No one knows those songs better than you," Sarah insisted.

"But I've never really done anything before. They're gonna want someone with lots of experience, I'm sure," Abbie explained.

"Look. The auditions are next month. Go and try out.

Chapter Four

What's the worst that can happen?"

"They could laugh in my face when I open my mouth! That would be pretty bad," Abbie replied.

"They're not going to do that," Sarah said as she watched Abbie's face drop. "Will you at least think about it?"

Abbie sighed. "Okay, I'll think about it. Come on, let's get that shake." The girls pedaled their bikes around the corner to the coffeehouse.

Chapter Five

When Kirk pedaled away from Abbie and Sarah, he headed straight for the library. If there were any articles about the lost gold shipment he would find them at the library. The microfiche of the local newspaper went back over a century.

Kirk entered the library twenty minutes later. There were only a handful of people there and most of them were senior citizens. This would be a perfect time to do some research.

The library had set up a computer database with a search engine for pinpointing information on the microfiche. The search brought up nine hits on news articles that contained the words "lost gold shipment." From the titles listed, he noticed two articles about the legend of the lost gold shipment that were specifically related to Albany. Kirk located the microfiche that contained the two articles. He quickly scanned the articles to make sure they would be useful to their investigation. Kirk printed them out to read more thoroughly later. The other articles appeared to be nothing of importance.

Kirk checked his watch. He hadn't told Abbie, but Kirk had an afternoon job two days a week. For the past three weeks, he had been sweeping, and carrying out the trash for Mr. Lawrence at his electronics and repair shop. He was earning twenty dollars a week, which was four times his weekly allowance. It was nearly four o'clock and time to go.

Kirk shoved the articles into his backpack and left the library. Mr. Lawrence's electronics shop was just a couple of blocks away. Kirk pedaled his way to Third Avenue in downtown Albany.

As he cut through the parking lot of the Snack and Fuel, Kirk encountered four boys from his school. He tried to avoid them, but Greg Schaeffer stepped into his path and Kirk had to quickly stop his bike to avoid crashing into him.

"Well, if it isn't one of the Hardy boys," Greg teased.

"Where's Nancy Drew? Out getting her magnifying glass polished? Huh?" James Porter sneered.

Kirk stayed silent. He knew that antagonizing them would only result in a black eye. He slowly inched his bike to the side of Greg Schaeffer, but Greg put his hands on the handlebars and stopped him.

Greg stared into Kirk's eyes looking for any sign of tears. "Where ya going?"

Kirk broke his silence. "I have to go to work."

"Work? You mean you have to go and play with your dolls, right?" Greg laughed loudly and the other three boys joined him.

"Can I go?" Kirk asked in an even tone.

Chapter Five

Greg got right in his face and sneered. "Yeah, you can go, but you remember something from now on. This corner is ours and we had better not catch you around here again. You got it?" He took his hand and slapped it against Kirk's shoulder to intimidate him.

"I got it," Kirk said softly.

"What? I couldn't quite hear you," Greg snapped.

I got it!" Kirk exclaimed. Greg stepped aside and Kirk fumbled with the pedals until he finally got his bike in motion. The boys were laughing and yelling names at him as he rode away. Kirk pedaled faster; soon their sounds faded.

Kirk's heart raced. When he knew he was far enough away from them, he stopped by a park bench. He threw his bike to the ground and kicked whatever he could find in disgust at himself. He wanted to stand up to those boys, but he was scared. Kirk tried to rationalize that it would have been four against one. He buried his face in his hands and fought back the tears. He was not going to cry over this. He wouldn't give those boys the satisfaction. Kirk took some deep breaths and got control of himself. He got back up on his bike and headed towards Mr. Lawrence's store.

When Kirk entered Lawrence Electronics and Repair Shop, Mrs. Lawrence greeted him with her usual kind face and smile. She was behind the counter, busy making out an order. "Good afternoon, Kirk. How was school today?"

"Not too bad. Sorry I'm late. I had to run by the library, and...I got a little delayed," Kirk wanted to tell her what had happened, but the last thing he wanted was for someone to feel sorry for him.

Chapter Five

"Well, you're just in time." The sound of something hitting the wall in the back of the store was heard. Mrs. Lawrence let out a heavy sigh. "Mr. Lawrence is having a little problem with his new computer. Can't you tell? Maybe you can give him a hand. You young folks are supposed to be pretty good with those things," she said.

"What's he trying to do?" Kirk asked as he rounded the corner of the counter.

Mrs. Lawrence put her hand on Kirk's shoulder, shaking her head in disapproval of her husband's crackpot ideas. "He has it in his head that we need a web page for the store. Says we'll double our business. I think he's wasting his time, but you know how he gets. Do you suppose you could give him a hand?"

Kirk grinned. "Not a problem, Mrs. Lawrence." Kirk stepped back into the office area where he found a very frustrated Mr. Lawrence. "Can I help?"

The old man looked up from his computer screen and a smile came across his face. "Kirk, my young friend, do you know anything about computers?"

"A little," Kirk replied with a grin. He sat down in Mr. Lawrence's chair and glanced at the computer screen. "Exactly, what is the problem?"

"It won't work!"

"No, I mean, what were you trying to do that doesn't work?" Kirk quizzed.

Mr. Lawrence took his handkerchief and wiped his brow. "I made this page about our store for the web and I was trying to upload it to the internet and it won't load."

Kirk moved the mouse around and checked the settings. He noticed where Mr. Lawrence had written down the logon and password on a yellow legal pad. Kirk signed on to the internet service and then made a few minor adjustments to the settings screen. He did one final check and pressed the enter button. "You're up."

"Just like that?"

"Just like that," Kirk confirmed.

"You're amazing!" the old man praised.

"Not really. I can also help you spruce up your page too. It's just some basic stuff I learned...oh, I mean the page you made is great but I'll be glad to..." Kirk couldn't finish his sentence. His boss had raised his hand to stop his explanation.

"Kirk, my boy. I believe that the internet is the way my store is going to grow. It's time for you to be promoted," he began. "I want you to fix up this website thing in addition to your sweeping and taking out the trash. Can you handle that?"

"With one hand behind my back," Kirk grinned.

Mr. Lawrence folded his arms. "Now, I suppose you will want a raise. I understand that these web people make a great deal of money." Kirk's face brightened and that stopped Mr. Lawrence in mid speech. He stammered a little and then continued, "I can't pay a lot, but..."

"You don't have to pay me, Mr. Lawrence," Kirk said calmly.

"Of course I'm going to pay you..."

An idea was hatching in Kirk's head. "I was thinking more of bartering," Kirk suggested.

Mr. Lawrence's face went blank at first and then the corners of his mouth raised a little to create a faint grin. "What kind of bartering did you have in mind?"

"My best friend and I have a sort of club. We like mysteries and all that stuff and we could really use a couple of cell phones," Kirk told him.

"Well..." Mr. Lawrence began.

"I figure that two of your cell phones and monthly service costs about sixty bucks a month. That should cover my services of web designing and maintenance."

Mr. Lawrence paced back and forth for a moment and rubbed his chin with one hand while he contemplated this proposal. Then he stopped, clapped his hands and held out one hand to make the deal. Kirk shook his hand and the deal was complete.

Kirk quickly swept the store and took out the trash. He would only have about a half-hour left to work on the website today, but tomorrow he would bring his digital camera and start making pictures of products in the store. By the end of the week, he would have Mr. Lawrence completely wowed by his design abilities.

Kirk worked diligently at the computer. Just as he was finishing for the day, Mr. Lawrence appeared in the office doorway carrying two small cell phones. "Here you go young man. They've been activated and here are the phone numbers."

"But Mr. Lawrence, these are the deluxe ones that have two-way radio capabilities. This is way too much."

"Not at all. You and your friend will enjoy all of the

extras on these babies. Now you head on home to supper. I don't want your folks to get worried about you," he replied.

Kirk shook his hand. He stuck the cell phones in his backpack and said goodbye to Mrs. Lawrence. About to exit the shop, Kirk stopped when Mr. Lawrence called back to him. "Oh, I almost forgot to tell you, Kirk. We're gonna close a little early on Thursday. We want to be home in time for the little trick-or-treaters."

"That's cool. I can be here right after school and do the sweeping and take out the trash before you close," Kirk replied as he swung his backpack over his shoulder. "See you tomorrow!"

Kirk was out the door and grinning like a possum. Abbie would go nuts when she saw the cell phones. Another thought came to Kirk. He laughed out loud and headed for the secret underground office.

Chapter Six

Abbie stayed longer at the Coffeehouse than she had intended. There were lots of kids hanging out there socializing. She enjoyed a heavily sugared cappuccino, instead of a milkshake, and a game of pool with Sarah. The Coffeehouse was the place to hang out after school and on the weekends. It usually had bands on Friday and Saturday nights and parents considered it a safe haven for pre-teens and teenagers to hang out.

It didn't take Abbie long to win the pool game. Her father started teaching her how to shoot pool when she was six. Frustrated, Sarah found a group of kids from school to talk to and Abbie went back to their table. She decided to read Mr. Strickland's report. It didn't take her long to realize that there was nothing in it that would be of any use to her. She was back to square one.

Abbie looked up at the clock on the wall and panicked. She couldn't afford to be late two nights in a row. If she pressed her luck she would definitely get grounded and not be able to attend Meredith's Halloween party on Thursday night.

Abbie's tired legs pedaled towards home. She lived in a neighborhood where the streets were lined with large, old trees that shaded the fading sunlight. The houses were a mixture of new and old homes. Abbie's house was built in the early 1950's and it was one of those homes that had a cozy lived-in feeling.

When Abbie turned into her driveway, she immediately noticed that her mother's car was gone. "Home free," she thought to herself. The lights were off in the front rooms of the house, which most likely meant that her dad was with her mother and she would have the house to herself.

Abbie entered the house through the back door. Just as she suspected there was a note on the kitchen table from her mom. Her parents had gone to visit a friend in the hospital and would be home around eight o'clock. Abbie set her backpack down on the kitchen table and located her dinner, which was on a plate in the refrigerator. She popped the plate of grilled chicken and vegetables in the microwave and set the timer.

Abbie grabbed her backpack and went upstairs. She changed into a pair of navy, fleece sweatpants and an Old Navy t-shirt. Since her parents were out of the house, she could take advantage of their absence and eat dinner in the family room in front of the big screen television.

Abbie went back to the kitchen and retrieved her dinner from the microwave and fixed herself a glass of iced tea. She took her dinner into the family room and made room for her plate on the coffee table. She clicked on the television and started surfing through the channels. It was almost time for prime time television to begin, so Abbie switched to the preview channel to check the listings.

Most of the channels had Halloween specials. She saw an advertisement for the Peanuts Halloween special, It's the Great Pumpkin, Charlie Brown. She made a mental note of its time and wondered if her parents would be home by then. Ever since Abbie could remember, she and her parents had watched the Peanuts Halloween special together. "Oh well," she thought. "Another tradition down the tubes." Abbie knew that if her dad had not been drug out of the house by her mother, he would be home to carry on the tradition. He would never forget.

Abbie found a rerun of Gilligan's Island, which was also a Halloween episode, and watched it while she ate her supper. The phone rang. Abbie quickly located the cordless phone and answered it to find Kirk on the other end.

"What's up, Kirk?"

"Oh, nothing much," Kirk replied.

"Did you find anything at the library?" Abbie asked as she continued to eat her supper. If her mother had been there she would be going nuts. Never was she allowed to eat and talk on the phone at the same time.

"I might have," Kirk replied smugly.

Abbie sighed. She just hated it when he played games. "Well?"

"I'll email the stuff to you later on, but first, I need you to go down to the office and see if I left my notebook down there. I'm 99.9% sure I did."

"What? Check it yourself. Charlie Brown comes on in fifteen minutes," Abbie replied as she gulped down another swallow of tea.

"I can't. I'm stuck at home. I really need to get a web address out of that notebook so I can finish up my report on the gold shipment and email it to you before you go to bed," Kirk explained in a calm tone. "So, if you would be kind enough to check on it for me, I would appreciate it."

"Okay," she huffed.

"Are you going right now?" Kirk quizzed.

"Yes, I'm going right now," she answered. "But if it's not where I can see it, I'll have to go back later after the show. I'm not going to miss Charlie Brown for your stupid old notebook."

Abbie hung up on Kirk and took another sip of tea before she went out to the greenhouse. As always, she carefully looked around to make sure no one could see what she was about to do.

Abbie pulled back the black plastic flooring and fumbled with the lock. She opened the hatch and climbed down the steps, pulling the hatch shut behind her. She flipped on the light switch and started looking around the office for Kirk's notebook. The little nerd had left it right next to the computer. "If Kirk's head wasn't attached to his shoulders, he would leave it somewhere too," she said to herself.

All of a sudden she heard a phone ringing. It wasn't the normal ring of the cordless phone used in the office. Where was that ringing coming from? Abbie followed the sound until she realized that it was coming from one of the filing cabinets. She opened the drawer and the cell phone rang again. Startled and a little cautious, she picked it up to answer it.

"Hello," she answered sheepishly.

"Surprise!" It was Kirk's voice on the other end.

"Kirk? What is this?"

"A cell phone, you ding-a-ling!" Kirk replied sarcastically.

"I know it's a cell phone, but what is it doing in my filing cabinet?" Abbie questioned.

"First of all, it's our filing cabinet and second of all, that is 'your' cell phone," Kirk replied.

Abbie was puzzled. She didn't own a cell phone. "Kirk, what's the joke here? I don't own a cell phone and you know that."

Kirk was pleased with himself. He had actually pulled one over on her. "It is yours now!" he replied. "I'm working after school for the Lawrences downtown. He asked me to design and maintain his web page, so we did a little horse-trading. Now we have cell phones for AGS Investigations. There's a sticker on the back with your number and mine."

"Kirk! I don't believe this!" Abbie was shocked. She didn't know what to say. "This is going to be great! But how am I going to hide it from my parents?"

Kirk was surprised at this remark. Abbie was one of the best people in the world at keeping secrets. "Abbie, you've hidden an underground office for almost three years. I think you can manage to hide a cell phone."

"That's true," she agreed. "Wow, Kirk. I really don't

know what to say. This is fantastic!"

"I know," Kirk replied smugly.

"So, do you really need that web address from your notebook?"

"No. It was just a ruse to get you down to the office and surprise you," Kirk laughed.

"Well, you definitely surprised me. Thank you, so much," Abbie said.

"I do have some information for you on the lost gold shipment. How did you do at the Old State Bank?"

Abbie's smile diminished. "Frustrating. I think that Mr. Strickland knows more than he's telling us."

"Well, I'm gonna email this stuff to you. You should have it after you finish watching your TV show." Kirk replied.

"Okay, I'll either email you back or just talk to you at school in the morning," Abbie said.

"See ya later," Kirk said as he hung up.

"Well," Abbie thought to herself. "The little nerd is going to be very useful."

Abbie stuffed the cell phone in her pocket. She secured the underground office and went back into the house. She finished her dinner and watched the Peanuts Halloween special, by herself much to her dismay. It didn't matter how many times she saw it, Abbie enjoyed every minute of it. Unfortunately, the end of the show meant the beginning of homework. What she had told Mr. Ed earlier was the truth. Sixth grade meant tons of homework every night.

Abbie took her dinner plate to the kitchen, rinsed it off and placed it in the dishwasher. She poured herself another glass of iced tea and climbed the stairs to her bedroom. Abbie unloaded her backpack and started her math homework.

Her parents arrived home at eight-thirty. Abbie took advantage of the break and went down to the kitchen for a refill of tea. When her parents came into the kitchen she chatted with them for a few minutes about her day and the big presentation. Her dad settled into his recliner to watch his nine o'clock show on TV and her mother had to make a congealed salad to take to work the next day. Her mother had started working at a pharmacy. It was the first time she had worked since before Abbie was born. Since there was nothing interesting happening downstairs, Abbie went back upstairs to finish her homework.

Just as Abbie finished the chapter in her history book, she heard the email signal from her computer. Abbie closed her book and tossed it aside. She clicked on the mail icon and sure enough, it was an email from Kirk.

"Okay, let's see what he found out," Abbie said to herself. She printed out the attachment and arranged the pages in order. She skimmed the article as she sat down on her bed, but didn't see any new information. Everything he sent was either information she already knew or things she had found out at the Old State Bank. Abbie was hoping for some incredible clue but nothing jumped out at her. Frustrated, she tossed the papers to the end of her bed, along with Mr. Strickland's report, and curled up with her pillow.

Abbie still had a little science left to read, but she could always do that in homeroom. She was tired and really didn't feel like doing anything else. For the past month or so, she had found herself getting tired easily. Maybe it was the stress of junior high. Her mom had warned her that at the onset of adolescence she would start feeling tired. If this was it, she would rather just hang a sign on her bedroom door that said, "Adolescent Inside: Do Not Disturb until after puberty!"

As she lay there, Abbie contemplated her Halloween costume. She had decided to be a cat, but she wanted to look cool, not like a little kid. She could modify last year's cat costume, but the overall costume needed something a little more daring...a little more grown-up. The solution hit her. Erin Nelson, a former babysitter of hers, had some really cool clothes. Erin was in the eleventh grade and probably had tons of stuff she had outgrown. She telephoned Erin and just as she thought, Erin was glad to help. They set a meeting time for tomorrow after school.

Now she was set for Meredith's party. Since the big high school football game was on Friday night, Meredith had chosen to have her party on Halloween, which was tomorrow, a school night. This meant an early curfew for Abbie. Oh well, it was better than trick-or-treating and this would be her first real boy-girl party.

Abbie also thought about emailing Becca. She hadn't heard from her in over two weeks, but that's the way it went these days. Becca had her life and Abbie had hers. They would always be friends, but a great distance separated them now and there was nothing that either one of them could do about that.

Abbie felt very sleepy. She pulled herself out of bed

and went over to her chest of drawers. She took off her navy sweat pants and put them away. Abbie brushed her teeth and picked out the clothes she would wear tomorrow. This would save her time in the morning.

Abbie pulled her covers back and crawled in under her sheet and comforter. When she switched off her lamp, the moonlight filled her room casting shadows on her as she stared out at the night sky. Within moments, she was fast asleep.

*   *   *

The dream began again. The dream that had haunted her for almost three years returned, its imagery stronger than ever. Once again, Abbie pedaled her bike as fast as she could. Other kids rode beside her, but she couldn't see their faces nor could she understand what they were saying. There were at least five people around her.

Tires squealed around the corner and the headlights silhouetted them. The car was getting closer and Abbie and the other kids tried to pedal faster. Suddenly one of the kids yelled something that sounded like Split up! and Abbie steered her bike to the left. She traveled across yards and between houses and down dimly lit streets.

It seemed as if she had been riding forever when she finally turned onto the dark dirt road. There were no cars in sight. The only images that Abbie could see were those of the trees and...a bridge just ahead. From behind the sound of the car approached and its headlights illuminated the road, casting large shadows in front of her.

Chapter Six

Abbie sat up quickly in her bed and gasped. She breathed quick short breaths as she looked anxiously around her room. It took her a few seconds to realize that it was only a dream. There were no cars, no headlights, no sign of danger. Her breathing slowed. It was only a dream, but this time she remembered more of the dream than ever. This time she understood. The eerie feeling of having been on the bridge in Crybaby Hollow before Tuesday was no accident. She had been there. The question now was...had it all been a dream or had it been real?

Chapter Seven

In elementary school, Halloween was one of those holidays that brought a great deal of excitement whether you were a kindergartner or fifth grader. However, junior high was a totally different ballgame. No one dressed up in costumes. Pumpkins and black cats didn't hang from the classroom ceilings. The day was just like any other day.

Instead of talking about what kind of costume they were going to wear, the kids talked about what they were going to do. Meredith's Halloween party was the topic of conversation. It was a total bummer that the party was on a school night and would end at nine o'clock, but since it started at six o'clock three hours were better than nothing.

In Language Arts, a few more students presented their projects but none of them kept Abbie's attention. Her mind focused on the lost gold shipment and its where-abouts. At the end of class, they discussed Washington Irving's Legend of Sleepy Hollow and its origin. By the end of class, the other kids had transplanted the story to Crybaby Hollow and deduced that the cry was from a child that the Headless Horseman beheaded. Just like Washington Irving, they had transplanted an old story to the hollow in Albany.

When the bell rang, all of the kids began filing out into the hall. Abbie went to her locker and unloaded the books she didn't need to take home and placed her history book in her backpack. Her history teacher, Mr. Jeffries was the only teacher that gave them homework.

As Abbie walked down the hall, she had the eerie feeling that everyone was staring at her. I'm getting as paranoid as Kirk, Abbie thought to as she continued down the hall. She hadn't gone very far when a girl she barely recognized from gym class said, "Nice picture."

Before Abbie could ask the girl what she was talking about, she was lost in the crowd of students trying to get out of the school. "That was odd," Abbie said to herself. Abbie shrugged it off and went down the stairs and out the exit doors to the bike rack. As she unlocked her bicycle, she could have sworn she heard a kid at the other end of the bike rack say her name...but she must be mistaken. Why would they be talking about her?

Abbie mounted her bike and started pedaling down the sidewalk towards Erin's house. Mr. Ed's grocery store was on the way, so she decided to stop there for her usual pack of M & M's and a root beer.

When Abbie came to a halt in front of Mr. Ed's grocery store, her eyes fixed on a shocking image. In front of her was the local newspaper stand and on the front page of the paper was a picture of her!

Abbie fumbled through her pockets searching for change to pay for a paper. She located two quarters, fed the machine its money and pulled down the rack to get a newspaper. As she pulled it out, a huge lump developed in her throat. Her face flushed and she felt a little lightheaded. Her worst nightmare had come true. She was the front page headline of the local newspaper.

Mr. Ed, who had apparently seen all of this from his store window, opened the door. "Come on in, Abbie."

Abbie was speechless. The thing she had tried to avoid since the first day of school was now totally out of control. It was worse than the summer headlines about the missing ducks from the Peabody Hotel in Memphis. While Abbie read the news article, Mr. Ed got her a root beer and a pack of M & M's. He popped off the top of the root beer and set it down in front of her.

"This is horrible, Mr. Ed. Just horrible!" she exclaimed.

"Why?" he replied. "Why is it so horrible?"

Abbie was almost at the point of tears. "I've been trying so hard to fit in at school...you know, be like the other kids and now they're just gonna make fun of me and..."

"So? Let them make fun of you if they want," he insisted. "If they do, they are no friends of yours to start with!"

"I know, but listen to this," Abbie replied as she started reading from the newspaper.

Chapter Seven

LOCAL YOUTH FINDS SKULL

Yesterday, Abbie Walker and a classmate at Albany Junior High, found a human skull in the woods at Crybaby Hollow. According to preliminary tests, the skull is that of a man approximately forty to fifty years old at the time of death. Further testing shows that the mysterious skull could have been in the woods for as long as twenty years or more. The skull is being transferred to the state forensic lab for further analysis. Identification of the remains is yet to be determined.

Many of you may remember that Abbie Walker and former Albany youth Becca Wallace solved the case of the missing ducks from the Peabody Hotel in Memphis, Tennessee, last summer. Their super-sleuthing skills led to the capture of the duck-nappers and the recovery of diamonds totaling..."

"I don't believe this. Is this legal? Can they just print my name in the paper like this and say that–"

Mr. Ed grinned. "Abbie, you are making a mountain out of mole hill. Look, you and your friend Tyler may have helped the police solve a very old mystery. Think of the family of this poor man, who may not have had any clue as to where their loved one has been all this time."

Abbie looked confused. Obviously, Mr. Ed had already read the story. She scanned the rest of the article and found where the reporter had cited the theories of the local police. One of these theories was that the skull belonged to a missing person. Other theories speculated foul play, but there were no apparent injuries to the skull. Investigators were combing the area for the rest of the skeleton.

"Maybe you're right," Abbie said with a little smile. She set the newspaper down on the counter and took a drink of her root beer. "You know, it's kind of funny."

"What that? Mr. Ed asked.

"My dad and I figured that it was just a practical joke for Halloween. I guess we were wrong," Abbie sighed. "Some super-sleuth I am, huh?"

Abbie picked up her M & M's as the front door to Mr. Ed's grocery store opened. To Abbie's surprise, Kirk came strolling in the door.

Abbie picked up the newspaper. "Have you seen this?"

"Uh huh. Okay, come on. I want to hear you say it," Kirk teased.

"Say what?" Abbie asked.

"Say...I made a mistake," Kirk announced.

Abbie laughed. "But Kirk, my dad and I..."

"Nope!" Kirk said louder. "Say it."

Abbie took a deep breath and ate her words. "I was wrong. I made a mistake. I should have listened to you when you wanted to investigate the skull instead of chasing after the lost gold shipment. Satisfied?"

"Thank you," Kirk said smugly.

"Can you believe this?" Abbie said in disbelief. She held out her M & M's and let some fall from the package into Kirk's palm.

"I had a funny feeling about that skull...so...while you were watching TV last night, I did a little searching on the internet," Kirk said proudly.

"And..."

"And, there are three missing person stories that fit in the twenty to forty years ago timeframe for the northern

Alabama area," Kirk reported.

"Really?" Abbie was intrigued. "I don't remember reading or hearing anything about people being missing."

Kirk sighed. "Well, I should hope not. You weren't even born yet." Kirk stepped back to the soda cooler and got himself a root beer.

"How long ago was the last one?" Abbie asked.

"Almost fifteen years ago," Kirk replied as he popped the top off of the root beer.

"Really..." Abbie contemplated this. Now she had a dilemma. This had the makings of a very interesting case. The only problem was, she and Kirk were already looking for the lost gold shipment. She knew they couldn't handle two cases at the same time.

"So, I'm thinking that we need to broaden our search of missing persons to include Tennessee, Georgia, Virginia–"

Abbie cut him off. "Hold up, Kirk. We're already on a case...remember?"

Kirk gave her a look of disgust. "Abbie, you need to face the facts. That lost gold shipment is a dead end. It's not here. Either someone found it and stole it a long time ago, or it never even happened."

Mr. Ed, who had stayed quiet during this discussion, butted in. "Oh, it happened all right. That you can be sure of."

Abbie toasted him with her root beer. "See! And Mr. Ed knows what he's talking about, Kirk."

"Oh, I'm not saying that you don't, Mr. Ed. I'm just trying to point out that there is no rush on the lost gold shipment case. The skull case is more exciting and..."

Chapter Seven

"And we should let the police handle it, Kirk," Abbie urged.

"I can't believe you're saying that!" Kirk exclaimed in disbelief.

"Well, I am," Abbie replied confidently. "This is out of our league."

Kirk's mouth dropped. "Out of our league? Out of our league! You've got to be kidding me! We've hunted down ghosts for a missing locket. You and Becca went up against diamond and duck thieves and were chased all across downtown Memphis! And, you think a skull is out of our league? I'm - I'm - speechless!"

"Well, that's a first," Abbie said sarcastically as she hopped off the stool. "I tell you what. Go ahead and investigate if you want to. Sarah's gonna help me look for the gold, okay?"

Shocked, Kirk replied, "Okay..."

Looking at the old clock on the wall, Abbie said, "But for right now, I have to go and see Erin about my Halloween costume, it's getting late."

"Then, I guess I'll see you later at..." Abbie stopped herself, realizing that Kirk may not have been invited to Meredith's party.

"At Meredith's house tonight?"

"Yeah. I'll be there," Abbie replied, relieved that Kirk had been invited. "What are you going as?"

"A mad scientist!" Kirk said in a low, growling voice. "And my friend Brian is going as Frankenstein's monster. What about you?"

"A cat," Abbie replied.

"Oh," Kirk said flatly.

"What do you mean by, 'oh'?"

"I don't know. I just thought you would have some really cool, creative costume...I mean are you going to come as Catwoman or –?" Kirk was interrupted by Abbie's hand, which cut him off.

"You haven't seen it yet...meow." Abbie teased in a sultry voice as she placed the money for her root beer and candy on the counter. "Catch ya later, Kirk."

Kirk looked to Mr. Ed, who was waiting for his response. Kirk shrugged and said, "Women."

*　　*　　*

Abbie had a perfect picture in her mind as to how she wanted to look for the party. She only hoped that her old black leotard would fit and that Erin Nelson's leopard skinned pants would fit her. Erin used to baby-sit her when she was little. If they didn't fit, she would definitely be up a creek.

Abbie pedaled towards Erin's house, which was just two blocks from Abbie's. She should have plenty of time to do her homework and get ready for the party. There would be no time to work on the lost gold mystery today. Her work-day was over and now it was time for some fun.

Chapter Eight

The pants fit like a glove. Abbie stood in front of her full-length mirror dressed in leopard-skin pants with a black long sleeved top that had a fancy sequined design on the front. Her black leotard had been entirely too small, but luckily, Erin had let her borrow a top to go along with the pants. She had made some cat ears to wear on her head and a long black tail, which she pinned carefully to the waistband of the pants. For a finishing touch, Abbie took an eyeliner pencil and drew some whiskers on her face. "Perfect," she said in a satisfied tone.

It was only four-thirty, so Abbie got out her history homework and started to work. Her mom would be home at five and her dad by five-thirty. The plan was for her Dad to drive her to the party. Meredith's house was in a new subdivision near the edge of town. Abbie had prepared herself for the lectures that would go along with a "boy-girl" party. She had been to lots of parties that boys had attended, but this was the first one in junior high and Abbie expected the worse from her mother. Then again, Dad might just be as bad on this one. She wasn't sure how her father was going to act, but she hoped he would be cool about it.

Abbie took another look at herself in the mirror. Tyler Graham would definitely take notice of her tonight. And...perhaps some of the other boys would as well.

Abbie worked diligently for the next half-hour and completed her homework just as her mother came home. When she heard the garage door open, Abbie closed her history book and walked downstairs. Her mother brought barbecue home for supper so Abbie could eat before going to the party.

Abbie posed in the doorway of the kitchen to surprise her mother. "Well, what do you think?" she asked as her mom entered the kitchen.

Abbie didn't get the reaction she had hoped for. Her mother's mouth fell open and she almost dropped the take-out bag from Gibson's Barbecue. Her mother was speechless and the excitement on Abbie's face turned into blank fear of what her mother was about to say.

"Uh..." her mother stammered. "I..."

"You don't like it," Abbie whimpered.

"No...it's not that I don't like it, honey...it's just that well...don't you think it's a little...grown-up for a girl your age?" her mother asked.

Abbie's eyes began to water. "No," she said flatly. "I thought it was pretty clever."

Her mother set the barbecue down on the counter.

"It is, Abbie," her mother replied quickly, very aware that she had hurt Abbie's feelings.

Abbie fell apart. She began to sob and through her tears, she found herself blurting things out to her mother before she even realized it. "I should have known you would hate it. You never like anything I do! I'll just stay home!" Abbie turned and ran up the stairs to her room, slammed the door and locked it behind her. She collapsed on her bed and buried her head in the pillows so she could cry alone in the privacy of her own bedroom.

*   *   *

When her father got home, he found a sack of barbecue on the kitchen counter, his wife sitting in the den crying softly and a front-page story about his daughter lying on the table in kitchen. He stood there, unsure of what had happened.

"She's upstairs crying," she began.

"About what?" he asked. "The newspaper?"

"No! It's my fault. She met me at the door wearing her Halloween costume and I...I guess I just wasn't prepared for her...to..." she sobbed.

"To what?" he asked in a worried tone.

"To look so grown-up!" she explained.

Abbie's father still couldn't put all of this together. "What was she wearing?"

"It's a cat costume," she began.

"That doesn't sound too bad."

Through her sobs, she managed to get out, "She looks like a cat in a nightclub act!"

"Oh," he replied with a smile and then an image struck him in the head of what Cathy was trying to convey to him and his "oh" turned to a concerned voice, "Oh! Uh... I'll go up and talk to her."

She stopped him by grabbing his hand as he walked past. "Tell her I don't hate it, I was just a little taken back. I mean I wasn't ready to see her..."

He looked down to her inquisitively. "How bad is it?"

Instead of answering him, she just motioned for him to go and see for himself. The steps up to Abbie's room seemed endless as he tried to imagine "how" his daughter was dressed.

He knocked on her door and there was no response. He knocked again and said, "Abbie, it's me. Can I come in?"

Abbie unlocked the door and sat back on her bed facing away from him. She didn't want him to see her crying out of control like she was three years old. Her dad walked into her room and when he saw her costume he let out a little laugh.

"It's not funny," Abbie insisted as she tried to fight back the tears.

"No, honey. I'm not laughing at you," he comforted as he sat down on the side of her bed and stroked her back. "By the way your mother was acting, I was just relieved to see your costume. I was imagining all kinds of things on the way up here."

Abbie turned to him with a look of surprise. "Dad!

Do you really think I would wear something that I would embarrass myself in?"

"No, of course not," he replied as he pulled her to him.

"I should have known she would hate it. I just thought that maybe she would–"

"Hold on a second," he interrupted. "You mother doesn't hate your costume."

"Really?" Abbie replied sarcastically and continued, "You could have fooled me. You should have seen the look on her face when she saw me."

"She was just surprised," he explained. "I mean leopard pants and sequins are a little different from what you normally wear."

"Dad!" she exclaimed infuriated. "It's Halloween! It's a costume! It's not like I'm wearing this stuff to school! Give me a break."

"I know," he agreed.

"I'm not trying to look trashy, just cool, you know?" she explained.

"I know," he replied. "Where did you get this get up anyhow?"

"Erin," she said.

"Oh, I see."

"What's that supposed to mean?" Abbie asked.

"Erin wears a lot of...interesting clothing," he explained.

"Dad! Erin is not a slut!" Abbie exclaimed.

"Whoa! I didn't mean it that way," he began. Her father looked away. "Boy, I am not ready for this." He put his head in the palms of his hands and rubbed his eyes.

Abbie let out a heavy sigh and dried the tears from her face. "Dad...hello! I'm not a little girl anymore. Whether you like it or not, I'm growing up and you have to trust me."

"I do trust you, honey," he said.

"Then tell Mom that I'm not trying to dress trashy... just cool. And another thing, I can't deal with the lecture she is gonna give me about boy-girl parties," Abbie said.

Her father looked surprised. "There are going to be boys there?"

Abbie sighed again, "Dad!"

"I'm just kidding," he laughed. "I know there are going to be boys there. And yes, I do trust you and so does your mother. You may not want to believe that, but she does. Abbie, you just have to understand that it's our job to be worried... to give you lectures about boy-girl parties and..." He stopped in mid sentence. He looked at her and grinned. "You've ruined your make-up. Need some help?"

"No," Abbie said as she sniffled. "I can do it. Will you go make peace with Mom?"

"I will go and talk to your mother, but you will have to make peace yourself," he told her. Abbie nodded and hugged her dad.

"Thanks," she said softly.

"I'll go and make you a sandwich. You can eat it in the car on the way over to Meredith's house," her father said. As he started to leave the room, he turned back to her, "Oh, by the way. Nice front page picture."

"You and the rest of the world," Abbie sighed. "Guess

74

Chapter Eight

we were wrong, huh?"

"Guess so," he grinned. "It's gonna be okay, honey. You'll see." Abbie's father kissed her on the head and went downstairs, leaving Abbie to fix her make-up.

Fifteen minutes later, Abbie and her Dad were in the car on the way to Meredith's house. Abbie's dad had smoothed things over with her mother and Abbie was able to leave the house without any more discussion on the subject of her costume or the party. Just as Abbie had expected, her father did offer his words of advice about junior high parties.

Abbie humored him as he talked to her about drinking and smoking. Abbie was well aware of these things, but she knew it made him feel better about the whole deal if he could just say it to her. Then, the subject she had been dreading... boys. Actually, her dad was rather cool about the whole thing.

He told her that he knew what it was like being a boy her age and this made Abbie want to laugh. She couldn't picture her father as a twelve-year old boy trying to impress girls. She simply said, "Yes, sir," after everything he said. And then, just like something out of The Brady Bunch he said, "I'm glad we had this talk." She wanted to burst out laughing in his face, but she didn't want to spoil his moment.

Chapter Nine

The talk was over. Abbie giggled to herself as she walked up to Meredith Fisher's front door. Abbie and her dad had always been able to talk about stuff. Her mom was a different story. It wasn't her fault though. Her mom had been raised in a household of non-communicators. For example, her mom learned about the "birds and the bees" from a book, because her own mother didn't like to discuss such things. Abbie had to give her mother some credit...she was trying. It was hard for her to talk openly with Abbie, and that's where her father came into the picture. Her dad was the youngest of four children. He had two older sisters, so very little embarrassed him. He was so cool about everything.

Today's talk was different, however. It didn't begin with "When you're older..." This time it was a little more nerve racking for her father since the when you're older was not in the future, but now! Did her dad really think she was going to this party just so she could make out with the boys? All of the things that were probably going through his mind made her feel sorry for him. But alas, it was just part of growing up...for him, that is.

Abbie rang the doorbell and Meredith answered the door. She was dressed in a genie costume, which was very cool. "You're late," she said as Abbie walked into the foyer.

"Issues with my costume," Abbie explained.

"Yeah, my mom was not exactly thrilled about mine, either," Meredith sighed. "She said 'proper young ladies do not show their navels.' Then, I pointed out that my navel is seen by everyone in Albany every summer at the pool. What's the difference?"

"And she said...?" Abbie questioned.

Meredith grinned. "She didn't have an answer for that one. So, what do you think?"

"You look fantastic!" Abbie replied.

"You do too. I love those pants, girl," Meredith said excitedly. "Come on, everyone's in the family room or out on the deck."

The girls giggled their way down the hall to the family room, which was filled with kids in costume. They were busy talking, shooting pool, and munching on a wide assortment of chips and candies that were laid out for them.

It didn't take long for Abbie to spot Sarah. She was outside on the deck. Abbie walked over to the sliding glass door and watched Sarah, who was dressed in a hippie costume, teaching a bunch of kids some swing dance moves.

There were several boys standing around waiting for their turn to dance with Sarah.

Just as Abbie was about to open the sliding door, Kirk and Brian jumped out in front of her on the other side of the glass, giving her a start. Kirk was dressed in a long white lab coat with a shirt and tie underneath. He had put some kind of gel in his hair to make it stand up straight as if he had been electrocuted. Brian was wearing a fabulous Frankenstein's monster outfit. The mask made him look just like the guy in the movie.

Kirk slid the door open as he and Brian laughed at the expression on Abbie's face. "Gotcha," he smirked.

"Very funny, Kirk Simpson. Ha, ha," Abbie replied with a little grin on her face. "Hi, Brian."

"Hey," Brian replied timidly. Brian Phillips was new in Albany. He had moved in over the summer and really didn't have many friends. He and Kirk had met at the library in August on Chess Day. They had hit it off immediately and been friends ever since. But Brian was very quiet. Even though they had invited him to come along to movies and other stuff, he never accepted. Abbie was glad to see that Kirk had gotten him to come to Meredith's party. Maybe this would help him come out of his shell.

Abbie looked around for Tyler Graham. Part of her wanted to hang out with him. She wanted him to see her costume and make a fuss over it. The other part of her just wanted to hang with Sarah, Kirk, and her other friends. As Abbie walked through the party saying hello to the rest of her classmates, she finally spotted Tyler. He was in a corner of the dining room with two seventh grade girls. He was talking and they were giggling. Abbie pretended she didn't see him and fixed herself a cup of Halloween brew, which was smoking from the dry ice.

For the next hour, Abbie and her friends danced and talked. She was trying not to think about Tyler and the two seventh grade girls. She knew he was like this. Why was she even surprised?

Mr. Fisher, Meredith's dad, had built a small bonfire in the backyard. Just as it was getting dark, he and Meredith called everyone to the backyard for the costume contest. The judges were Meredith's mom and dad, her older sister and her boyfriend. All of the kids that wanted a chance to be judged in the contest, paraded across the end of the deck one at a time.

While Meredith's mom counted up the judge's votes, her dad gathered everyone around the fire for a round of ghost stories. He began to tell them about the old Robinson house that used to be on the south bank of the Tennessee River. It was one of the few structures that didn't get burned during the Civil War. The large antebellum home was used as a hospital by both sides during the war.

"During the winter months," he said as the fire crackled, "the ground would get so hard that they couldn't bury the bodies of the soldiers that had died. So, they started burying them in the basement because the dirt floor down there was still soft. I even heard from one of the old timers around here that they dug tunnels out from the basement towards the front lawn to make these rooms to...stack the bodies in. Pretty soon, they got afraid that they were digging out too far, so they started stacking the bodies in the basement like firewood. It was cool enough down there to keep the bodies until spring and the ground outside thawed."

Several of the girls grabbed on to each other as if they were frightened out of their wits. Abbie sighed. If they thought this was scary, they would never have survived meeting Caroline, a real ghost girl, last June. They would have fainted dead away. This story was a baby's bedtime story compared to what she had been through.

"So the years passed, and the war ended. The Robinson family fled with the other Albany citizens when the Yankees marched into town, and they never returned. The house was sold to one family after another. No one stayed in the house for more than a year. It sat empty more often than not." He stopped, leaving the story hanging out there for the kids to think about.

"And...?" one boy asked finally after a long silence.

"Why did no one want to stay there?" another girl asked. With this question, Meredith's dad was flooded with questions about the Robinson house.

He continued, "Family after family reported seeing soldiers walking the halls. Some saw nurses leading soldiers from room to room by candlelight. They heard wailing in the middle of the night as if someone was in horrible pain." The kids around him winced. "My favorite story is one of a young boy who was sleeping in his bed. He had been ill with a high fever and his mother had just left him alone for a few moments to get a cold washcloth for his forehead. The boy was lying there, waiting for his mother to come back, when suddenly he felt the presence of someone in the room. He looked up and saw a wounded soldier standing at the foot of his bed. The boy, unsure of whether or not he was dreaming, closed his eyes for a moment and then opened them again. The soldier was indeed standing there, staring at him. The boy screamed!" Girls around him shrieked out at his sudden outburst.

Mr. Fisher never smiled. He looked very serious as he continued with the story. "The boy's mother came running into the room at the very same time the soldier walked out of the room. She didn't see the ghost of the wounded soldier that night, but...instead, she felt his icy cold presence walk through her body as she entered the room."

Gasps and giggles flooded the group of kids gathered around the bonfire. The corners of Mr. Fisher's mouth turned up slightly as he started sticking marshmallows onto his stick. Mrs. Fisher let out a loud whistle and all the kids settled down.

"I have the results of the costume contest!" she bellowed. "This was a hard decision and like it or lump it we have the winners!"

Cheers erupted from the kids gathered around the bonfire. There were several unruly boys making muffled comments. Abbie was thankful that Mr. and Mrs. Fisher couldn't make out the snide things they were saying about the contest.

"For the third place winner, we have this sack of Halloween candy," she said holding up a large orange paper sack with a jack-o-lantern design on the front. "The third place winner is Jennifer Williams!"

Jennifer stood up quickly and several girls around her gave her high fives as she ran up to the front. She was dressed as Dorothy from The Wizard of Oz. No originality here, but the costume was perfect in every detail.

"The second place winner receives two movie passes and a coupon for popcorn and drinks at the Movieplex," Mrs. Fisher continued. "The second place winner is Tyler Graham!"

Abbie gasped as his name was called out. Tyler was dressed as Elvis and as he approached Mrs. Fisher he put on the Elvis moves. Seeing him do this reminded Abbie of her summer visit to Memphis where she saw a number of Elvis impersonators pretending to be Elvis on just about every street corner. Abbie clapped and whistled along with the other kids as Tyler took his prize and did an Elvis pose for the crowd. All of the girls swooned over him, much the way girls used to do over Elvis when he was alive.

As the cheering settled down, Tyler held up his hands and said in his best Elvis voice, "Thank you. Thank you very much." The crowd applauded as he went back to his seat. Several girls called out offers to him to go along to the movies. Tyler pretended like he was writing down their phone numbers and making dates with all of them as his friends pulled him back down to the ground.

"And now, for the grand prize - first place in our costume contest. The winner receives a twenty-five dollar gift certificate to be used at any store in the mall...drum

Chapter Nine

roll please..." The kids began to beat their hands against their legs to create the sound of a drum roll. "It's a tie! The winners are Kirk Simpson and Brian Phillips!"

The kids exploded with more applause mixed with yells and whistles. Again, the group of boys that had been so unruly before were yelling out things like, "Let's hear it for the nerds!" and "Who invited them?"

Abbie shot them a glare and proceeded to yell louder than anyone else in support of her friends. "Way to go Kirk! Brian!" She whistled and screamed until her throat hurt. Kirk and Brian timidly went to the front and retrieved their prize. They both managed somewhat of a bow and a wave as they headed back to their seats. Abbie pushed her way through the crowd to them.

"Congratulations!" Abbie exclaimed.

"Wow! Can you believe it?" Kirk said surprised.

"I can't believe you guys actually won," came a voice from behind them. It was Sarah, who was obviously quite perturbed that she wasn't one of the winners.

"Just lucky, I guess," Brian replied as he looked down at his feet.

"Well, I suppose you guys deserve it. I mean your costumes are great," Sarah conceded. "But watch out next year boys, Sarah Martin's gonna beat'cha." Sarah flipped her hair back over her shoulders and pranced over to another group of girls who were preparing to roast marshmallows.

"So, do you think Tyler's gonna be mad that he didn't win?" Kirk asked.

"Oh...no, of course not. Knowing Tyler, he probably

thought the whole thing was really silly. I'm sure he doesn't care," Abbie replied before realizing how it must have sounded to Kirk and Brian. "Uh...not that it is silly. I mean, I don't think it is. I think it's great. But you know how Tyler and those other guys are..."

"Yeah, I know what you mean," Kirk replied. Brian was being very quiet. He wasn't used to being around this many people in a social setting. He was mostly looking down at the ground as Abbie and Kirk talked to one another.

"Well, I'm gonna roast myself a marshmallow. You guys want one?" Abbie asked.

"Maybe later," Kirk replied. "I want some more punch. I'll be right back."

"Sure," Abbie said. Kirk walked away towards the deck, leaving Brian there alone with Abbie. She had not spent a lot of time around Brian and really didn't know what to talk to him about.

Brian held his monster mask in one hand and was pushing his hair out of his face with the other. The mask, along with the heat from the bonfire, had made his head sweat. Abbie had no idea what to say to him, but she had to say something. This was getting very awkward.

"So, how do you like Albany so far?" she asked.

Brian looked up slightly. "I like it okay, I guess. But, I wish I was back in Chicago."

Abbie remembered now that Brian had moved to Albany from Chicago. "Really? You miss the big city?"

Brian sighed. "Yeah. There's more stuff to do there and my friends are there."

Chapter Nine

"You've made friends here. I mean Kirk's your friend. I'm your friend." Abbie was proclaiming her friendship to Brian even though she really didn't know him that well. She just felt sorry for him.

"It's so different in Chicago. You can just exist and do your thing and nobody's keeping up with what you're doing," Brian explained.

"Yeah, in a town the size of Albany, everyone knows what everyone's doing all the time," Abbie agreed. "It can get really annoying."

"My aunt still lives in Chicago. My mom says that were going to go back for a visit during the Thanksgiving break," he said happily. This was Brian's first real smile Abbie had seen all night.

Kirk approached them holding the remains of his punch. "What'cha guys talking about?"

"Chicago," Abbie replied as Greg Schaeffer and his buddies butted in on their conversation.

"Well, well, well. Looks like Super Geek and his sidekick bagged first place," Greg teased.

Kirk and Brian stayed quiet and stared at the ground. Abbie detested Greg Schaeffer, who had been a thorn in everyone's side for too long. "Ha, ha," she smirked. "What are you supposed to be?"

"We're rappers," Greg replied. "Can't you tell? Oh... no of course. They don't have rap music in the form of show tunes."

"Well, we can certainly thank God for that now, can't we?" she snipped back at him.

Chapter Nine

"Yeah, well, when you decide to stop hanging around the freaks and geeks, we'll be glad to have you hang with us," Greg laughed. "And, by the way, great costume." He gave her a thumbs up and a leering grin.

Chapter Ten

At the moment Greg turned around he came face to face with Tyler Graham who had walked up behind him. Greg's expression changed immediately. He stammered a little and managed to get out a hesitant, "Hey, Tyler."

Tyler shoved him away. "Got a problem, Greg? Pestering my friends again?"

Tyler Graham's remark caused Greg to cast a shocked look at Abbie, Kirk and Brian, who were also totally surprised. As far as Kirk and Brian knew, Tyler had never said more than two or three words to them. However, Kirk quickly came to the conclusion that the Tyler's statement of friendship was only due to the fact that Abbie was with them.

Greg regained his composure and said, "No, Tyler. No problem. We were just heading out." Greg and the other boys eased away from Tyler until they quickly disappeared into the crowd of teenagers.

"Thanks," Abbie said.

"Like they said, 'no problem'." Tyler replied in his Elvis voice. "Oh, and as for you two..." Kirk and Brian looked nervous. "...great costumes."

The boys smiled. They were relieved that Tyler wasn't going to give them a hard time about them winning first place. Abbie grabbed Tyler's arm and pulled him over to the side. Kirk and Brian tried not to look in their direction. Abbie obviously wanted a moment alone."

"Thanks," she whispered.

"Greg's a pain," Tyler grunted. "A bunch of us are going to play Capture the Flag. Wanna come?"

"I can't," Abbie replied reluctantly. "My dad's gonna be here in fifteen minutes."

"Bummer," Tyler said.

"But, could you do me a favor?" Abbie asked.

"Sure. What?"

"Would you ask Kirk and Brian to play?" Abbie pleaded.

Tyler's expression went blank. "Uh, I don't know..."

She tightened the grip on his arm. "It would be a big favor to me. Brian's new and hasn't made many friends. It would be very nice if you invited them to play since you just told Greg they were your friends."

Tyler surrendered. "Okay. As smart as they are, maybe they'll have some strategy ideas to help us beat Don and them."

Abbie smiled at him and said, "Thanks again."

As she let his arm go to turn around, he stopped her.

"Since I'm doing you a favor, then would you do me one?"

"Uh...okay," Abbie replied.

"Come with me to the movies Saturday afternoon?" Tyler asked.

Abbie blushed. A real date with Tyler Graham? Could this be? Her mom would definitely freak about this. "Well, I'm not allowed to go out alone with a boy until..."

Tyler raised his hand to stop her. "Tell your parents they'll be a bunch of us. It's a group thing."

Abbie let out a small sigh of relief. Her parents would buy that. "Then...yes."

"Great," Tyler smiled. "We're meeting at the Movieplex at two o'clock."

"I'll be there," Abbie whispered, though inside she really wanted to shout it out to everyone at the party.

Tyler turned to Kirk and Brian. "Men, we have a mission. A bunch of us are going to play Capture the Flag and I need both of you on my team if I'm gonna beat Don Jones. What do you say?"

Kirk and Brian's mouths dropped. Kirk was the first to answer. "Absolutely!"

Tyler, Kirk and Brian walked away leaving Abbie standing by herself.

Abbie watched the boys walk off to join the rest of the kids who were getting ready to play Capture the Flag. She wanted to join them very badly, but her dad would be there to pick her up soon. After the afternoon she experienced with her mother, the last thing she wanted to do was make it worse by not being ready to leave the party on time.

Chapter Ten

When Abbie turned around, she almost ran over Sarah who was standing directly behind her. Sarah had a flat expression on her face. Abbie immediately realized that Sarah was unhappy about something. Before Abbie could ask, Sarah opened her mouth. "So, what were you and Tyler talking about?"

Abbie was stunned. Had those words really come out of Sarah's mouth? Flustered, Abbie looked over her shoulder in the direction of where the boys had gone and then turned back to Sarah. "Uh...I was just asking him to include Kirk and Brian in the Capture the Flag game," she stammered.

Sarah's expression didn't change. "Really?" she questioned suspiciously.

"Yeah," Abbie said defensively. "What's the problem?"

"Nothing," Sarah said in an expressionless tone.

"No...what is it, Sarah?" Abbie pleaded. Sarah just looked down at her shoes, not wanting to continue this conversation. Abbie wasn't going to let her off the hook that easily. "Sarah. Bryan was telling me about how much he missed his friends in Chicago and it just kind of hit me that Kirk is his only real friend here. I just thought it would be a good thing for Tyler to include both of them."

Sarah broke her silence. "Tyler's hanging out with Kirk?" Sarah's eyebrows raised in complete doubt of the legitimacy of this claim. "Why would Tyler Graham want to be seen with Kirk Simpson?"

"Because I asked him to do it as a favor to me," Abbie explained. "Greg Schaeffer and his dimwit friends are giving Kirk a hard time and I thought it would help

Kirk out a lot if he hung around with Tyler some. Might scare those other stupid boys away."

"Oh," said Sarah.

The girls walked up to the deck by the back door. Neither girl said another word to each other as they opened the sliding glass door into the family room of the house. Abbie got a little ahead of Sarah and she felt Sarah's hand on her shoulder urging her back.

"Hey," Sarah began. "Sorry. I didn't mean to–"

Abbie interrupted her. "You should have told me that you liked Tyler."

"Hello!" Sarah exclaimed. "Are you blind? Every girl in the sixth grade likes him."

"So why were you giving me a hard time?" Abbie asked, completely and utterly confused.

"I...don't know," Sarah said looking away again. "It's just that I'm really not close friends with any of those other girls and I just thought you were...like...stabbing me in the back."

Abbie sighed heavily. "Look, Sarah. I guess I'm just like the rest of the girls. I do like Tyler. There, I said it. But," she paused long enough to turn Sarah's face directly towards her so that she could look her in the eye. "Tyler is my friend. We did a project together. We've talked on the phone once or twice. Saturday, I may go with him and a bunch of other kids to the movies. None of this means we are 'going together.' He hasn't asked me and he's not gonna ask me. He's not going to ask anyone. He's just not the kind of boy that has one girlfriend."

Chapter Ten

Sarah continued to stare into Abbie's eyes even after Abbie finished talking. She curled her bottom lip and bit it. After what seemed like an eternity, Sarah said in a shaky voice, "You're going to the movies with him?"

"Uh!" Abbie grumbled. She turned away from Sarah, went to the table that had the party favor bags filled with Halloween candy. She snatched one up and started walking for the front door. When she had almost exited the room, she turned back to Sarah. "Well, do you want to come on Saturday?"

Sarah's face brightened almost immediately. She simply nodded and smiled at Abbie, who waved goodbye to her and headed out the door for the front curb. Her dad was there waiting for her - right on time.

Chapter Eleven

Capture the Flag is one of those games that everyone learns at summer camp or perhaps with the other neighborhood kids. Neither Kirk nor Brian had ever gone to summer camp or played with neighborhood kids, so Tyler had to explain it to them.

"The game is similar to a game of chess or war. Each team has a flag that is made of whatever material the team can come up with. Usually, the flag is attached to a broom handle or long stick found in the woods. The teams draw out boundaries of where their territory is and they hide the flag somewhere inside those boundaries," Tyler explained.

"That doesn't sound too hard," Kirk said.

"It gets better," Tyler continued. "Each team gets fifteen minutes to hide the flag and plan how they're going to protect it. The object of the game is to sneak into the other teams territory and capture the flag without getting captured themselves. Any team members tagged by the opposition are frozen in place and must stay put until the end of the game. When a team member captures the flag of the opposing team they have to bring it back to the middle of "The Clearing" to a designated point to claim victory."

"For tonight's game," Meredith spoke up, "I have put a purple hula hoop that glows in the dark on the spot where Tyler and Don had agreed."

The two teams were situated in a large clearing behind Meredith's house. Her neighborhood backed up to a wildlife refuge that contained hundreds of acres of woods along the Tennessee River. "The Clearing" as everyone in the neighborhood referred to it was always busy with kids practicing one sport another. Families enjoyed afternoon picnics and kite flying on Saturday or Sunday afternoon with warm weather.

As soon as Tyler finished explaining the game, Kirk knew exactly why he wanted them on his team. Both Kirk and Brian were excellent chess players and strategy was their middle name.

Tyler's team was composed of twelve girls and boys and their headquarters was a short walk into the woods nearest one end of the subdivision. Don Jones' team had an equal number of players and they headquartered themselves on the opposite side of The Clearing inside the woods that bordered the wildlife refuge. Both teams were in their territories plotting and planning how they were going to capture the other team's flag. Tyler let Kirk run the show and stood back, impressed at Kirk's ability.

Kirk was used to Abbie being in charge and wished she was there, but he knew this was his chance to show everyone what he could do. Kirk assigned Heidi Cook to be the Watcher. Her job was to stand guard over the flag, but as Kirk soon learned, the rules stated that she could not be any closer than twenty paces. Therefore, Kirk told Tyler to position Heidi at the correct distance from the flag and hide her. He then proceeded to assign another girl and boy, who he didn't know, to hide at other points of entry into the woods in case Don's team got past the front lines.

With the flag protected, Kirk gathered the remaining eight players around him in a huddle. They bent down to the ground and using a flashlight, Kirk drew the playing field and territories in the dirt with a stick. Kirk sketched out a plan for four of them to sneak into Don's territory and capture their flag. Tyler, Kirk, Brian and Meredith would head up this offense. The rest of the players, which included Sarah, were assigned to defensive positions that would protect their territory from Don's team.

Instructions given, they all piled their hands one on top of another to show that their team was united and ready to play. As they stood up, Tyler put his hand on Kirk's shoulder. "Man, you need to help us with our football plays."

Kirk only smiled back at him. For the first time in his life, Kirk felt like one of the guys. More than anything, he wanted to capture the other team's flag and bask in the glory of being on a winning team that included some of the most popular kids in school.

Chapter Eleven

There were no lights in The Clearing. Only the moonlight, the stars and a few lights from the back porches of scattered houses gave any illumination. The further away from the subdivision they got, the darker it was. It became so dark, Kirk had to squint very hard to even see his own hand in front of his face. Suddenly, a whistle rang out from the other side. That signal meant that the game would begin in one minute. Tyler called out, "Let's go," to his team members and they all moved into position - the positions that Kirk had assigned them.

As Kirk advanced slowly and quietly, he imagined himself running though the field triumphantly carrying the other team's flag. Don't count your chickens before they hatch, he thought to himself. Cautiously, Kirk moved forward, trying to keep low and not bring any attention to himself. If he were going to capture the other team's flag, he would have to circle around behind and come in from an angle that they wouldn't expect.

Kirk saw motion ahead of him and dropped to the ground. It was definitely one of Don's team members. He couldn't tell if it was a boy or a girl in the darkness, but he or she moved past him without realizing that he was only a few feet away from their path. Kirk looked to a far edge of the woods. That was his spot of entrance. He squinted hard to see if he could make out any other moving shapes between himself and the woods. There were none that he could see, so he decided to proceed. If all was going well, Brian was doing the exact same thing on the other end of the playing field.

Kirk knew that their flag was at least a five-minute

walk into the woods. How far into the woods had Don hid his team's flag? Kirk thought to himself as he inched his way to the woods. He needed to hurry. If Don's team got through their front lines, it wouldn't take long for them to capture the flag.

Kirk was allergic to grass and after crawling for hundreds of feet, he had this dying urge to sneeze, but he couldn't. A sneeze would give him away for sure. Finally, he reached the edge of the woods. As Kirk looked into the trees, it was as if he was peering into a large room with no windows. The woods were pitch black. How would he ever find the flag?

Beneath his feet he could hear the crunch of twigs and dried autumn leaves. Each step was a guessing game. He had no idea what was ahead of him. Slowly, his eyes began to adjust to the new level of darkness and he could now make out the trunks of trees. At least now he wouldn't be running into them. He so wanted to take out his flashlight and shine it through the trees until its beam hit the target, but he didn't dare.

Kirk continued deeper and deeper into the woods. The chill of the night had created a low-lying fog. He felt like he was on the set of a horror movie and that at any time the Werewolf or Count Dracula would jump out from behind a tree. Even though, Kirk didn't scare that easily, he was feeling a bit creepy. He stopped for a second to get his bearings and suddenly realized that he had gone so far into the woods that he could no longer see The Clearing behind him.

Chapter Eleven

You are not lost, he kept repeating to himself in a very low whisper. In the distance he could hear an owl. Kirk reasoned with himself that he had been walking in a fairly straight path since he entered the woods. If he simply turned back to his left, he should end up in the vicinity of the other team's hiding place for their flag - or at least close to it, he hoped.

Kirk imagined a layout of the subdivision, Clearing and woods in his mind. With the Clearing directly behind him, Kirk took a deep breath. He turned to his left and started walking in the direction that he prayed would take him towards the flag. He hadn't heard any cries of victory from anyone, so at least there was still a chance.

Kirk came to a large pine tree and stopped to lean against its trunk for a quick rest. He took out his nerd's handkerchief and wiped the sweat from his face. It definitely wasn't hot outside in the night air, but he was wearing several layers of clothing and he always perspired when he was nervous or anxious. Kirk leaned his head back against the tree and looked up to the night sky. The thickness of the trees in the woods made it hard to see the stars but every now and then he could make out a group of them through an opening in the...Kirk gasped. Were his eyes deceiving him? Hanging from the crook of a tree just a few feet away was what appeared to be Don's team's flag. Kirk focused harder on the object and then realized that there was no mistake about it. Their flag had been made from the hood of Don's ghost costume, which was now attached to the end of one of Meredith's mom's broom handles.

Chapter Eleven

Where were the Watchers? Kirk wondered. They had to be out there somewhere, just waiting for him. Holding his breath, Kirk stared into the woods, looking in all directions for any sign of a Watcher. Had they all deserted the flag and went after their team's? Had the Watcher fallen asleep or gotten bored? There was only one way to find out.

Kirk stepped cautiously towards the tree. He fully expected someone to jump out at him and tag him...but no one did. The flag was his for the taking. Kirk hugged the tree and shinnied up its trunk, just high enough to reach the broom handle. Carefully, Kirk lifted the flag out of its nesting area and quietly slid to the ground. Now, the question was...did he go back the way he came - if he could find his way back that way or did he head straight for The Clearing and start a dead run for victory?

Kirk pondered his options for a minute and then decided that his geometry teacher was correct - the shortest distance between two points was a straight line! He put one foot in front of the other and headed in what he hoped would be the right direction. Just as Kirk reached another large tree, he began to see moonlight ahead. The Clearing was out there.

Suddenly, Kirk heard a branch snap behind him. The Watcher was back there and would soon realize that the flag was gone. Kirk started walking again, but this time he moved a little faster. The anxiety of making it in time caused him to move faster than he really wanted. More sounds from behind. They were after him.

Kirk broke into a blind run. His shoulders and his

arms bumped into trees as he tried to escape from enemy territory. Just when he thought the edge of the woods was in sight he felt his feet hit something hard and his legs buckled as he plummeted to the ground. He had fallen over a log. There was a pain in his knee where he had come down hard onto the broom handle that held the flag. Kirk couldn't worry about a little pain right now. He had to get up and run!

Kirk pulled himself up and started towards The Clearing again. Just a little more he kept telling himself as he limped faster and faster. As if he was breaking out of a large bubble, he found himself in the open air. No trees in his way. Victory was directly in front of him! The full moon had risen even higher since the start of the game, and Kirk could see things much clearer now.

To his left, Kirk saw someone approaching quickly. It was the enemy. It had to be. Run faster! he kept telling himself. To his right, Kirk saw something strangely familiar. The moonlight was bouncing off a large amount of sequins. It was Tyler's Elvis costume!

Taking a chance, he shouted, "Tyler? Is that you? It's me, Kirk. I've got the flag! I've got the flag!"

The sequined figure stopped and Kirk slowed his pace. The enemy to his left was closing in and Kirk knew he couldn't run any more. There was only one thing to do.

Tyler, who had been trying to figure out where Kirk's voice had come from, spotted him and called out, "Kirk! It's me! It's Tyler!"

The enemy was almost upon him. Kirk screamed,

"Catch, Tyler!" As the words left his mouth, so did the flag leave his hand. He hurled the broom handle like a javelin towards Tyler.

Tyler caught it and like a football pass, pulled it close to himself and started running. Kirk screamed, "Run!", then the enemy tackled him, sending him to the ground. The pain in Kirk's knee grew worse. Don Jones had tackled him but Kirk felt as though it had been a truck. Every inch of his body was beginning to ache.

Don apologized for being so rough and helped Kirk to his feet. Seeing that Kirk limped, Don helped him towards the center of the field where a large group of kids had gathered. Half of them were shouting and screaming with excitement over their victory. Tyler had planted the broom-stick in the center of the glow in the dark purple hula-hoop ring. When he saw Kirk approach, Tyler shushed everyone.

"And here he is! My main man, Kirk Simpson, who captured this flag and like a seasoned quarterback threw me a pass that I wish every one of you could have seen. Let's hear it for Kirk!"

Both teams clapped and shouted praise for Kirk, who had suddenly forgotten about his pain. The joy of winning and being included wiped it all away...that is, until he took another step. Pain shot up his leg like a bolt of lightning. Several of the other boys helped him take his weight off the bad knee.

Tyler looked at him and grinned. "Now you can say you've got an old football injury!" The other kids around him laughed and Kirk too laughed through his pain.

The party was over and all of the kids started heading back towards Meredith's house. For the lucky ones who had been able to stay later, their parents would probably be waiting on them. Kirk wished that Abbie had been there to see their victory. Ahead, Kirk could see Sarah.

"What happened to you?" she asked in a sympathetic tone.

"I fell in the woods and then I got tackled," Kirk explained.

"Are you okay?" she questioned.

"He'll be all right," Tyler assured her. "We just need to put some ice on his knee."

"You guys did great!" Sarah exclaimed, trying to change the subject.

Both of the boys replied with a thanks, and then Tyler spoke up, "Kirk here should get all of the credit." "No, Tyler. You're the one that made it to the center," Kirk pointed out.

"I was just finishing what you started," Tyler replied.

Kirk didn't answer Tyler. He let Tyler's words hang there as they slowly walked up to Meredith's backyard.

When they reached the deck, Sarah went inside to get an ice pack. Kirk pulled up his pants leg to reveal a nice goose egg on his knee.

When Sarah came back with the ice pack, Kirk gently put it on his knee. The pain was horrible, but he didn't dare let Tyler see him wince. He gritted his teeth and forced a smile. The only kids left on the deck were Kirk, Tyler, Sarah and Meredith. Everyone else had either gone home or was waiting out front for their ride.

It suddenly occurred to Kirk that he hadn't seen Brian since the game started. He looked around and then turned to Sarah. "Have you seen Brian?"

Chapter Twelve

The phone rang. Abbie awoke with a jolt. She looked at her clock and saw that it was 1:56 a.m. Abbie sat up on her knees and held her breath. She reached over and turned on her lamp. A phone call in the middle of the night meant a prank call or a wrong number or even worse - an emergency. From the feeling in the pit of Abbie's stomach, she knew something was terribly wrong.

She heard footsteps as her father or mother walked to her door. Goosebumps rose on her arms as she watched her door silently open. It was her father and from the expression on his face, she knew. Their eyes locked and his solemn face told her before he even uttered a word.

"It's Kirk," he began. Abbie couldn't breathe. She couldn't speak. "Kirk...needs to talk to you."

Relief. Abbie had been afraid that something horrible

had happened to Kirk, but she knew now that it was something else. She was able to take a breath and the chill bumps subsided. Abbie picked up her cordless phone and mashed the talk button. Her father stood in the doorway of her bedroom, watching and waiting.

"Kirk, what's wrong?"

Kirk's voice was shaky. "Abbie...he's gone!"

"Who's gone?" Abbie pleaded.

"Brian. Brian's missing," Kirk said.

Abbie could tell by the sound of his voice he had been crying. "What do you mean missing?" she questioned. "After we played Capture the Flag, Brian wasn't there. He's vanished. His bike is gone and his mom hasn't heard from him, and no one saw him leave and–"

Abbie butted in, "Kirk! Check the bus station. He may be on his way to Chicago."

There was silence on the other end of the phone. Finally, Kirk responded, "Chicago? Why would Brian go to Chicago?"

Abbie took a deep breath. She didn't want to tell him all of the things that Brian had told her at the party, but now there was no choice. "Kirk, listen to me. At the party tonight, Brian told me he was unhappy here and wanted to go back to Chicago. He has an aunt and friends there and well... Kirk, just tell his mom that. He's probably at the bus station or hitchhiking or I don't know... Just tell them, okay?"

Kirk said, "I will," and then there was a click. He was gone. Abbie mashed the talk button again and laid her phone on the table beside her bed. She looked up at her father.

Chapter Twelve

"Brian's run away," she said softly. There was a trace of guilt in her voice. If she had just told Kirk or someone, maybe Brian wouldn't have done this.

"Hey," her father said gently, and sat on the edge of her bed. "Don't beat yourself up over this. There is no way that you could have known Brian would do this."

"But, I..."

"No. There's nothing you can do," her father reminded her.

"I should help them look," Abbie said in a determined voice.

"Absolutely not. It is the middle of the night and the only thing you are going to do, my little super sleuth is to go back to sleep," her father ordered. "Brian's mother and the police will handle it from here, and I would be willing to bet you a month's allowance that Brian will be at home safe and sound by morning."

Abbie started to speak again but her father put his finger to her lips to stop her. He tucked her in and kissed her on the forehead. After her father had walked from her room, she rolled over towards the clock and watched the minutes click away. It was sixteen minutes after two. She thought of Brian out there in the dark by himself. Was he hitchhiking? Was he staring out the window of a bus somewhere between here and Chicago? She sniffled and a tear ran down her cheek.

"I should have told somebody," she whispered to herself. Her eyelids became heavy and she drifted off into a dreamless sleep.

Chapter Thirteen

Friday, November 1st

When you're a little kid, you play this game called Gossip. It's a really stupid game where you sit in a circle and someone whispers something to the person next to them and then they turn and whisper it to the next person and so on. By the time it goes all the way around the circle, the thing that the person said in the beginning is all twisted and just completely wrong.

I feel as though I've just been through an eight-hour game of Gossip. School today was horrible and I'm not exaggerating. When I got to school this morning, I knew Brian wasn't going to be there.

Don't ask me how I knew this, but I just knew. Kirk, who is never late to school, checked in during third period. He and his dad had been up most of the night driving around Albany looking for any sign of Brian.

When Kirk came into third period, he looked like he hadn't slept in days. He should have just stayed at home. Every kid in the entire school was talking about Brian and what really makes me angry is that yesterday NO ONE was talking to Brian. He was just another nameless kid to everyone but Kirk. Now, with rumors of kidnapping and running away from home and the other crazy stories of why he is missing, all the kids at Albany Junior High are making Brian out to be like their best friend of something. Poor kid had to run away to get anyone to notice him.

I'm worried about Kirk. We only talked for a few minutes today. He just looks so sad...and I don't know what to say to him. I feel so sorry for him. I know what it's like to lose a friend...kind of. I mean, when Becca moved away I had a hurt in the pit of my stomach that lasted for days and days and days, and I knew exactly where she was. This must be much worse for Kirk. Brian was his closest guy friend and –

Chapter Thirteen

The hatch to the secret underground office opened. Abbie laid her journal and pen on the desk. It was Kirk. He climbed down a little ways and closed the hatch above him, then stepped down the rest of the ladder.

When he turned towards Abbie, his head was down. Abbie didn't know what to do or say, but she managed to get out, "Any news?"

Kirk shook his head and walked over to his desk and set down his backpack. He stood there, with his back, to her and took out a notebook, a map and some file folders. Without turning around, he said, "I went to the County Records office today. They made me some copies of a map that shows the woods behind Meredith's house all the way down to Crybaby Hollow. Then I picked up a map that shows all of the interstates and highways between here and Chicago."

Abbie stood up and walked over to his side. She looked at the maps that he had spread out on top of the desk. He was using his finger to trace the roads out of Albany towards Illinois. Abbie placed her hand on top of his and stopped him.

"Kirk...I know you're upset. I know you want to run out there and walk every inch of road between here and Chicago, but it won't do any good. Brian's run away and the only thing you can do for him right now is...well...pray."

"You don't understand," Kirk muttered.

"I do...a little," she comforted. "When Becca moved away, I felt like someone had kicked me in the stomach, I..."

"It's not the same," Kirk said sharply. "Brian didn't

get in a car and move away, he left, he..." Kirk grabbed the map and crinkled it up as tears streamed down his face.

Then, Abbie did something she never thought she would never do in her whole entire life. She put her arms around him and hugged him. "I'm sorry, Kirk. I'm so sorry," she said softly. "You're right. I don't know how you feel. I can't."

She let go of him and went back to her desk. She felt a tear slide down her cheek and she knew that if Kirk saw her crying it would just make him feel worse. Abbie pulled out her research on the lost gold shipment and started reading over the information Kirk had gathered for her.

Kirk was using highlighters to mark all of the possible roads from Albany to Illinois. He pulled out the bus schedule he had gotten at the bus station and studied it. He discovered that there was no bus to Chicago that left from Albany. If Brian had left by bus, he would have had to go to Birmingham first and then wait until tonight for a bus that would take him to Chicago. Kirk dismissed a bus trip as a possibility. If Brian had done this, the police would have found him by now.

He pulled out the maps of the woods behind Meredith's house. There were four of them. The oldest one dated back to just after the Civil War and the other three were updates that were done about forty years apart.

Both of them worked in silence for the next half-hour. Abbie reread the four articles about the lost gold shipment. The information was sketchy at best. Just the same old story told over and over again. Frustrated, Abbie closed the research file and took out Ray Strickland's paper he had written in college. She remembered that the paper detailed the historical events around the date the gold shipment came up missing. And, even though Mr. Strickland's close attention to detail was great, there was nothing in the paper that she didn't already know. Abbie hoped that there was something she had missed, but after giving it another read, she felt like she was back to square one again.

Abbie swiveled around in her chair to face Kirk. She had to get his mind off of Brian. "Hey," she said breaking the silence. Startled, Kirk looked over his shoulder. "I was just thinking that maybe you could take a break and help me on the lost gold shipment case. I'm at a dead end, I think."

Kirk looked at her, contemplating his answer.

"Sorry. I just can't concentrate on anything else right now."

"Oh, sure," Abbie quickly replied, trying not to sound insensitive. "I understand."

There was an awkward silence and Abbie turned away from him. A few minutes passed and Kirk turned to her. "You wanna take a break from that case and help me on this one?"

Abbie froze. What was she going to say to him?

"Uh, well...I'll..."

"That's okay. Forget it," Kirk snapped.

"No, look, I'm sure that–"

"Just stop, okay," Kirk said coldly. "I know you think he's just a runaway, but I don't believe it. Something happened to Brian last night and I seem to be the only one that sees that!" Kirk had raised his voice so loud that by the time he finished, Abbie was scared to say anything to him. He picked up his research and shoved it into his backpack. Without saying anything else to her, he climbed the ladder, opened the hatch and in a huff, left the secret underground office.

Abbie knew there was no use going after him. He was upset and mad at the whole world. She had just pushed the wrong button with him and she needed to let him cool off. Abbie opened her journal and picked up where she had left off.

Kirk just left the office. He's mad at me right now and I'm gonna let him cool off before I try to reason with him and make him understand that Brian is most likely on his way to Chicago via his bike.

I am at the end of my rope with this lost gold shipment case. Everywhere I turn there's a dead end. But, I feel like I'm over-looking something important. It's like there's a clue staring me in the face and I can't see it.

Tomorrow is Saturday and I'm going to the movies with Tyler and a bunch of friends. Since I was out late last night, I've promised my parents that I'll stay home tonight. One of my mom's friends is coming over for supper. I'm positive it will be a boring dinner followed by boring conversation in the living room, followed by me going to bed early.

I'm going to email Becca tonight and fill her in on everything that's happening. I can't believe I haven't talked to her in weeks.

Abbie closed her journal and shut down everything in the office. Supper was scheduled for six-thirty and it was almost six o'clock now. She needed to hurry and get up to the house before her mother started looking for her. It wouldn't do for her mom to discover the underground office. Not yet.

Chapter Fourteen

Abbie was right. Friday night's dinner was very boring. But, Abbie knew the expectations of "the parents." She had to mind her manners and make polite, thoughtless conversation. However, the food was delicious. Her mother had gone all out to impress Dianne, her supervisor at work.

Her mom had taken a job at the beginning of the school year at a local pharmacy. Before Abbie was born, she had worked as an assistant in a pharmacy, but quit to stay home with Abbie. Now that Abbie had started junior high, Cathy Walker had decided to return to the workforce.

Abbie knew her mother had told her about Dianne, but now that she was sitting across from the lady trying to make polite conversation, she couldn't remember too much about her. Every now and then, her mom would pass off a little fact about Dianne and add on, "Remember, I told you that?" Whenever this happened, Abbie just nodded and smiled.

There were a few things about Dianne that Abbie could remember. She was in her late sixties and had been a practicing pharmacist since she was twenty-five, although these days she was semi-retired.

"Abbie," her mother began. "Dianne's family has had a drugstore in Albany since the turn of the century."

"Which one?" Abbie asked sarcastically before she realized how the tone of her voice sounded.

Fortunately for Abbie, Dianne thought it was funny. Her father joined the laughter a few seconds after Dianne, but her mother didn't even crack a grin. She only glared at Abbie.

"Actually, my father started Palace Drugs and Soda Shop in 1924," Dianne explained proudly.

"Oh," Abbie replied politely, trying to look interested.

"Dianne started working there right after college, isn't that right?" Cathy added.

Dianne wiped her mouth with a blue linen napkin and returned it to her lap. "That's right. My father worked there until the day he died. Had his heart attack right there behind the counter while counting out pills."

This caught Abbie off guard. She wondered if Dianne had been there when he died or if she had found him, but she was scared to ask. She only managed to say, "I'm sorry."

"No, it's fine...really. He died doing what he loved... helping people," Dianne sighed. "I miss the old place sometimes."

Jonathan Walker jumped into the conversation. "Oh, me too. I have great memories of my father taking me downtown when I was little. We'd go to the Palace and have a thick milkshake and sit at the bar on those stools that spun around and around. It was the highlight of my Saturday. And then remember your sister Laurie and the 'Loo-Hoo's, how they used to..."

Abbie watched her mother give her father an eyebrow-raised cold look of disapproval and he halted the conversation about her Aunt Laurie. Crazy old Aunt Laurie was a taboo subject in the Walker household.

Her father cleared his throat and continued, "No one has ever made a better milkshake!"

"We had the best milkshakes in town," Dianne bragged.

"It's a shame that all those downtown stores are closed," Cathy said returning to her polite voice and smile.

"Yes," Dianne nodded. "Makes me wish I hadn't moved the business out to the Parkway. I should have stuck it out downtown."

"It would be nice if some developer would revitalize the downtown area and open up little specialty shops," Abbie's mother suggested.

Her father's face lit up like a Christmas tree. "Wouldn't it be great to have the Palace open again? Even if it was just an ice cream shop!"

Dianne smiled. "Yes, it would, but I'm afraid it's a lost cause. These days, people want shopping malls, strip malls, big fancy steel and glass buildings. They just don't want old and classy."

Chapter Fourteen

These words hung in the air like a thick cloud. Everyone at the table sat in silence. Dianne was right, but no one wanted to agree with her. Cathy finally broke the silence and suggested coffee in the living room. Abbie gave her mom a pleading look of wanting to escape upstairs to her room, but her mother's glare told her she was trapped for a little while longer.

Abbie's mother fixed a pot of coffee and they sat in the living room, or as Abbie referred to it "the white room." This was the most useless room in the entire house. It was decorated to the hilt and no one was allowed to go into it, especially with food. Dianne's visit was important enough to allow the "no food or drink" rule to be lifted. As Abbie sat down in the wingback chair, she remembered the prank that she and her father had played on her mother a year ago. As a gag gift for Christmas she and her father took a series of pictures of themselves in the "white room" with food, drinks, and dirty shoes propped up on the arms of the chairs and couch. Her mother had not been amused with their brand of humor.

In an effort to ease the tension, Abbie's mother said, "Abbie, tell Dianne about the project you did for class on Crybaby Hollow."

Abbie rolled her eyes at her mother, but without too much coaxing, she began to tell Dianne all about her and Tyler's video report on Crybaby Hollow. Dianne set her coffee down on the end table and laughed as Abbie ended the legendary story.

"Oh my dear, that brings back memories, let me tell

you," she laughed. "No telling how long the stories of that bridge have been told around these parts."

"Tyler and I interviewed some folks that have been around for a long time," Abbie said.

"You did talk to Ed Norman, didn't you?" Dianne quizzed. "He–"

"Oh yeah, we did," Abbie quickly interrupted, much to the dismay of her mother. Then, she realized she hadn't asked Mr. Ed about Crybaby Hollow. She had only asked him about the lost gold shipment. "Uh, no. I was mistaken. I was going to interview him about it, but we just ran out of time," she explained. "Actually, my friend Sarah and I went to see him the other day to ask him about something else."

"Really?" Dianne asked intrigued.

"Yeah, one of our classmates did a report on–"

This time, Dianne did the interrupting, but Abbie's mother didn't glare at her for doing it. "Let me guess. You were asking him about Miss Kate and that handsome river-boat captain, Simp McGhee."

"Uh, no," Abbie replied. She had never heard of these people. "We talked about the lost gold shipment that..."

Again, Dianne went wild with excitement. "Why of course! I should have guessed. Heaven sakes alive, daddy would have loved to have told you all about it."

"Really?" Abbie's face brightened.

"Oh my, yes," said Dianne. "My daddy made the study of that missing gold his hobby for most of his adult life. My mother told everyone he was on some mission from God to find it. He was the authority on the subject in these parts, that's for sure."

Abbie felt like she was on a game show and she had just won the grand prize. "You're kidding me. That is so cool. My friend Sarah and I went to the Old Bank the other day, and another friend Kirk, did some searching for information at the library, but to be honest, we haven't turned up much."

Dianne chuckled. "Of course you haven't. People who have turned up clues are certainly not going to share them with the world, just in case the gold is really out there."

Abbie noted the skepticism in Dianne's voice. "So do you think it's really out there somewhere or just an old legend?"

Dianne didn't respond at first. She picked up her coffee cup, took a sip and then set it back on the saucer. Quietly, she continued. "My daddy spent most of his life searching for that gold. He never found it. No one did. But he went to his grave believing it was still out there, somewhere."

She paused and Abbie wasn't sure how to proceed. She sat there, waiting for Dianne to make the first move. "I tell you what," Dianne continued, "If you're really interested, I'll let you go through my daddy's papers and all of his research."

"Really?" Abbie asked excitedly.

"Only if you promise me one thing," Dianne insisted.

"What's that?" Abbie asked.

"Promise me you won't spend your whole life looking for it," she said. "Don't let it turn into an obsession like my daddy did."

"No, of course not," Abbie agreed though she wished

she could hide her hands behind her back and cross her fingers as she made the promise.

"Oh my. Where are my manners? Here I am making plans with Abbie and I should be asking you first. Cathy, Jonathan, is this okay with the two of you?" Dianne asked apologetically.

Abbie's mom nodded her head, "Oh of course it's okay with us. Isn't that right, honey?"

Abbie's dad was caught off guard a little, but quickly agreed with his wife. "Sure. Sounds like a lot of fun. But I hope you know what you're in for with this one."

Abbie beamed with excitement. She knew she looked like a little kid wanting to open her presents on Christmas morning.

"It'll be fine," Dianne said in a pleased voice. "Can you find some time around two tomorrow? I'm afraid it's then or sometime next week."

"Yes!" said Abbie enthusiastically. "That would be great for me!"

"Good. Meet me in front of the old Palace at 2:00 sharp tomorrow. You might want to wear something that you don't mind getting dirty. The old place is full of dirt and dust and there's a lot of stuff to go through."

Abbie was bursting with excitement. She was so excited she almost forgot to ask where the old Palace Drug Store was, but then she remembered to ask. "Now, exactly which building is that?"

"Oh yes. I guess you're too young to remember where the old Palace was," she said. "It's on Bank Street right down the street from the Old Bank. In fact, if you stand on the steps of the Old Bank building, and look down Bank Street, it will be the first building on your right in that first row of buildings."

"Okay, I know where you're talking about," said Abbie. "Should I just meet you out front?"

"That'll be fine," said Dianne.

"I didn't know you still owned the building," said Jonathan curiously.

"Oh I couldn't sell it," Dianne injected. "My great grandfather built it just after the Civil War. It was a grocery store back then. It just has way too much sentimental value."

"Of course," agreed Abbie's mother.

"Now I just use it for storage. But, I left my daddy's office just the way he left it. Didn't see any point in boxing everything up, when that was my favorite place in the world to be. Sometimes I go down there and sit for hours reading his journals and books. He used to read them to me when I was a little girl." Dianne was lost in a memory of the way things used to be and it touched Abbie to see how deeply she was still connected to her father.

Abbie was beaming from ear to ear. Deep down she knew there were more answers tucked away in that old building. Her imagination ran wild with the possibilities of what could be down there. Realizing that she needed to call Sarah and update her, she decided to excuse herself from the conversation. She thanked Dianne, said goodnight to everyone and sprinted up the stairs to her room.

The first thing on her agenda was to call Sarah. Then,

she would call Kirk and tell him the good news. Maybe it would cheer him up. Abbie picked up her phone and dialed Sarah's number. It rang for almost a dozen times before Sarah finally answered.

"Hey, it's me. For a second there, I thought you weren't home," said Abbie.

"No, I was just waiting for a commercial to come on," Sarah replied.

Ditzy Sarah, Abbie thought to herself. "Okay...well, I've got some great news."

"Tyler asked you to go with him," Sarah said excitedly.

Abbie grumbled, "No, Sarah, nothing like that. I think we finally have a break in the case. My mom's boss, Miss Dianne, has tons of information on the lost gold shipment. So, tomorrow, I need you to go with me downtown to meet her at 2:00. I'll come down to your house around 1:30, so we'll have time–"

"Abbie! We can't do that. We're meeting Tyler and everyone else at the movies tomorrow," Sarah reminded her.

Abbie's heart fell. "Oh no! I can't believe this! I totally forgot about that. Sarah, what am I gonna do?"

"Well, duh, just tell this Dianne lady that you'll have to meet her earlier or some other time," said Sarah.

"No, I have to meet her tomorrow at 2:00. It's the only time she has this weekend," said Abbie.

"So, we meet her on Monday after school," Sarah suggested. "What's the big deal?"

"I can't wait that long, Sarah. I have to know what's in those journals," Abbie insisted.

"Then you'll have to call Tyler and cancel," said Sarah.

"But how am I going to do that? What do I tell him? I can't tell him I'm working on a case," Abbie reminded her.

"Just tell him that something suddenly came up," said Sarah.

"That's the stupidest thing I've ever heard of in my life. What kind of excuse is that?" Abbie said.

"It worked on the Brady Bunch," said Sarah.

Abbie sighed. "Why don't you go to the movies with them. I..."

"Uh uh," Sarah said quickly. "I wouldn't feel right doing that. Besides, I want to come with you to investigate."

"Okay, I'll call Tyler and tell him that 'something suddenly came up.' But, I can't believe that he'll buy that," Abbie said skeptically.

"It'll work. Trust me," said Sarah.

This assurance from Sarah didn't make Abbie feel any better. "Tell you what. Why don't you ask your mom if you can spend the night and we'll watch movies and pig out tomorrow night?"

Sarah was stunned. She hadn't spent the night with Abbie since they were eight years old. Overjoyed, she accepted, saying that her mother would be very cool with that. The girls hung up and Abbie worked up the nerve to call Tyler. As she was dialing she hoped Tyler wouldn't be home and she could just leave a message, but he answered the phone.

She told him that something had suddenly come up and he said okay without asking any more questions. They postponed the trip to the movies until the next Saturday.

Chapter Fourteen

That was easy, Abbie said to herself. Abbie changed into a nightshirt, brushed her teeth and climbed into bed. She really wanted to email or call Becca, but she decided to wait until after she had investigated the old Palace Drug Store. After tomorrow afternoon, there would be loads more to tell her.

Chapter Fifteen

Abbie and Sarah arrived at the old Palace Drug Store shortly before two o'clock on Saturday afternoon. Sarah wore a pair of dark sunglasses and a hat to disguise herself. She didn't want anyone to recognize her while she was wearing grubby clothes.

Dianne arrived at 2:00 on the dot. The large black Cadillac pulled into a parking space directly in front of the old building. Dianne got out of the car wearing a pair of faded old jeans and a long sleeve flannel shirt.

"Afternoon, ladies," Dianne greeted them on the sidewalk.

"Hey," Abbie greeted. "Dianne, this is my friend, Sarah Martin."

"Nice to meet you," Dianne said cheerily. "Are you girls ready to get dirty?"

Abbie answered before Sarah had a chance to

respond. "Sure. A little dirt never hurt anyone."

Dianne laughed and took a ring of keys out of her purse. She unlocked the front door to the Palace and told the girls to stay at the doorway until she turned on some lights. Abbie and Sarah could barely see anything ahead of them. The tall front windows were covered with dark brown butcher paper and the sunlight from the open doorway just wasn't enough to illuminate the darkness.

A few minutes later, the girls heard the distinctive sound of the main breaker being turned on and soft lamp-light filled the main room of the old Palace. At least half a dozen chandeliers hung from the ceiling. They were covered in cobwebs and though some of them only had a few working bulbs, it was enough light for Abbie and Sarah to see the layout of the old drugstore.

There was a main counter that had about ten barstools like the ones her father had described. They had tattered, dusty burgundy seats with stuffing sticking out from the gashes in the vinyl. There was a large mirror behind the counter with an ornate frame around it. The world "Palace" was written in large script above the mirror with the inscription "established 1897" written below it. The old ice cream shop equipment was still there and Abbie could imagine how shiny all of it must have once looked.

The rest of the main room had small chrome tables and chairs where people used to sit and have their ice cream treats. The seats of the chairs were the same burgundy vinyl as the barstools. Everything in the room was covered with several layers of dust and dirt. In the back of the room, there was another counter for the drugstore part of the shop. The girls could see rows of display cabinets and shelving where all of the items for sale in the pharmacy had once been.

Dianne appeared in the doorway by the drugstore counter. "Well girls, right this way." She motioned for them to follow her and Abbie and Sarah carefully walked to the back of the room. Just past the doorway to the back, Dianne went down a set of stairs to the basement.

"Ooo," Sarah whispered to Abbie. "I don't know if I want to go down there. It's gonna be gross and full of spiders and rats and–"

Abbie grabbed Sarah's arm and squeezed it. "Hey! You wanted to work with us on investigating right?" Sarah nodded sheepishly. "Okay then. Get a backbone and come on."

Sarah was not happy with this and she made a face at Abbie but followed her anyway. They walked down a set of wooden steps that were lit by three single light bulbs that were hanging about four feet apart from each other on the path down the stairs.

At the bottom of the stairs, Abbie could see lots and lots of stuff sitting around on the floor. It looked like the leftovers from about two dozen garage sales, but none of this really interested her. What she wanted was straight ahead.

In the middle of the junk, there was another door leading into a separate part of the basement. Dianne had already opened the door and was inside the office picking up piles of papers and books from two leather chairs. When Abbie and Sarah stepped into the office, they were amazed at the difference between the office and the rest of the building. It was well lit and clean as though it was still being used on a daily basis for a working office. The large room had bookcases lining one wall and old steel filing cabinets lining the opposite wall. There was a large dark wooden desk at one end of the room and a conference table directly in front of that. More leather bound chairs circled the table that had neat piles of books, files, pictures and newspaper clippings.

The next thing Dianne said made Abbie laugh. "You'll have to excuse the mess. I've been scrapbooking."

Mess, Abbie thought to herself. This was one of the cleanest, most organized offices she had ever seen. "No, this is absolutely amazing."

"Your father sure had a lot of books," Sarah said in amazement.

Dianne proudly looked around at the collection. "I loved his collection of books. I cannot tell you the hours of pure joy I experienced in this room." Dianne sat down in one of the chairs at the conference table. "When I was a little girl, my father would be working upstairs, so I stayed down here in the office reading and entertaining myself. These books took me away to the most marvelous places I could imagine."

Abbie and Sarah surveyed the bindings of the books to find everything from classics to more contemporary writers. There were reference books and history books and both fiction and non-fiction books.

"Well, I know you girls don't have all day, so let me show you what I've got about the lost gold shipment," Dianne said as she walked over to one of the filing cabinets. She picked out a small key from her key ring and unlocked one of the four drawer filing cabinets. She took out a large journal that was at least three inches thick and several files that had newspaper clippings hanging out the edges. She brought them over to the conference table and cleared out a space for Abbie and Sarah to examine them.

"This is my father's journal about the lost gold shipment," Dianne explained.

"That whole thing is just about the lost gold?" Sarah questioned.

"It sure is. My father recorded everything in this journal," she said tapping it gently. "These files are filled with newspaper clippings and copies of documents about the shipment."

"Wow," Abbie said amazed. "This is a lot of stuff."

"I told you," Dianne said. "It'll just take you time, but I think you'll find it interesting." The sound of her cell phone interrupted her and she took it out of her purse to answer it. "Hello? What? You have to be kidding me? No, tell them not to leave. I'll be right there." Dianne looked disgusted. "Well, girls, I have to run. I just bought some new furniture for my den and the delivery truck is at my house. Fools weren't supposed to deliver it until Monday."

Abbie's heart sank. She didn't want to leave. She was so close to so much information.

"Will you girls be all right if I leave you here for a little while?" she asked.

"Sure," Abbie replied.

"I shouldn't be gone more than an hour," explained

Dianne.

"Or we could lock up for you. We can bring the keys by your house or–" but Abbie was interrupted by Dianne holding up her hand.

"I have a better idea," she stated as she walked over to the large executive desk. "Here's an extra set of keys. When you get ready to leave, just turn out these lights and there's a light switch by the front door that will turn off the lights upstairs. I can turn the breakers off tomorrow. Then, just lock the front door and take the keys home to your mother and she can bring them to me on Monday. How about that?"

"Not a problem," Abbie replied taking the extra set of keys.

"Okay. Oh...and I'm going to lock the front door so nobody can get in up there," she said as she gathered her things.

"Thank you, Miss Dianne," Sarah said politely.

"Yeah, thanks a whole lot," said Abbie.

Just as Dianne was walking out the door, she called back to them, "I hope you find what you're looking for... and if you do, remember, I get half!" Her laughter died away as she walked up the stairs to the first floor.

Abbie opened the large journal, while Sarah started going through the files that contained news articles. The journal was Dianne's father's handwriting but fortunately his penmanship was fantastic. The first date of entry was June, 1934. Abbie skimmed the first entry and noted that Dianne's father, Peter Sullivan, had discovered the story of the lost gold at the age of thirty and decided to start a quest for it.

The first five or six pages recorded conversations he had with old timers of the day. Since the shipment had been missing for almost seventy years in 1934, even these personal accountings were just hand-me-down information. Everyone had a story of what they thought had happened and Peter Sullivan had taken the time to document every single person's idea or opinion.

Sarah found news articles dating back to 1914. Every five or ten years, someone had done an article about the lost gold shipment just to keep it on everyone's mind. There were articles poking fun at those people who had dug up their yards looking for it, but still, no new information.

Abbie read sections of the journal out loud and Sarah took notes of anything they felt was interesting or new. This went on for over and hour and a half and by that time they were getting weary.

"You know, Kirk should be down here with us. This is right up his alley," Sarah protested.

"Yeah, I tried to call him this morning, but there was no answer at his house," Abbie replied while still reading to herself from the journal.

"Too bad he doesn't have a cell phone. We could just call him," Sarah said.

Abbie had forgotten all about the cell phone. It was in her backpack pocket. She looked up from the book and over at Sarah who was on her third file of newspaper articles and documents. She needed to call Kirk, but if she did, she would have to reveal the cell phone to Sarah. Oh well, she thought to herself. Sarah's gonna find out sooner or later.

Abbie opened her backpack pocket and took out the cell phone. She turned on the power and it made a beeping sound.

"Hey, when did you get a cell phone?" Sarah asked in surprise.

"Oh, the other day, actually. Kirk has one too, but until you said something about it, I had totally forgotten..." she was dialing and trying to act very nonchalant about the cell phone business. She let Kirk's phone ring several times and finally, she got his voice mail. "Hey Kirk, this is Abbie. Sarah and I have made a great paper discovery on the lost gold shipment. We're on Bank Street in an old building. When you get this message, give me a ring. Bye, bye."

She pushed the "end" button and laid the cell phone on the table. "Maybe he'll call us back in a little while–" Before she could finish her sentence, her cell phone was beeping.

"That was quick!" Sarah exclaimed.

"No, it's not ringing, it's my voice mail," Abbie said. She pushed the "message" button and it said, "You have three messages." Abbie punched in her secret code and the message began playing back:

"Abbie, this is Kirk. It does not do us any good to have cell phones if you don't leave yours ON! Anyway, it's early Saturday morning and my dad and I are going to hang up some more posters with Brian's picture on it on the highway leading out of town. You never know. Something might turn up. Talk to you later. Give me a call when you get this message."

Abbie erased that message and started the next:

"Abbie, oh my gosh. Please call me as soon as you get this message. They found Brian's bicycle down by the river near Riverside Park. The police are down here and they're gonna start dragging the river...to see if Brian..." Kirk's voice was breaking up because he was starting to cry. "I tried you at home, but no one answered. Call me... okay?"

A chill ran through Abbie as she erased the last message. The sound of Kirk's voice was loud enough through the earpiece that Sarah heard every word he had said. She looked at Abbie with sad eyes. Abbie thought she was about to cry, but both girls were in a state of shock. The third message began to play. It was Kirk again and Abbie dreaded what he was about to say.

Chapter Sixteen

"Abbie, it's me again. I don't know where you are, but please call me when you get this message. I really need to talk to you. They're still dragging the river, but they... they haven't found anything yet. My dad is staying here, but I'm going back to...well you know, to do some research. I have an idea of what might have happened to Brian, but..." Kirk's voice was gone. Evidently he had gone into one of those gray areas where he didn't have a strong enough signal to transmit. Just as Abbie was about to punch the number seven to erase the message, she heard him say, "I think he could have..." and then he was gone for good. The display on her cell phone read "call ended."

Abbie looked at Sarah. "We have to go."

Sarah understood. They had to go to the river and see if anything new had happened. Kirk was probably back from the office and down there too. Abbie tucked the journal under her arm and they headed for the office door.

"Hey, you can't take that!" Sarah said stopping her.

"But I'm not finished yet," Abbie replied.

"So? You can't just take her father's journal without asking. That's just wrong." Sarah was correcting her. Abbie shook her head. This was a first.

Ashamed of what she was doing, Abbie replied, "Look, I know I shouldn't but I'm at a really good place in the journal. There's something about the tunnel from the river to the Old Bank. We'll go check on Kirk and then we'll bring the book back later. Dianne won't even be down here until tomorrow afternoon anyway."

Sarah reluctantly agreed. Abbie carefully put the large journal in her backpack and zipped it up. They closed up the basement and walked to the top of the stairs. They turned off the upstairs lights and locked the front door. She put her backpack on and the girls mounted their bikes and started pedaling toward Riverside Park.

They rode down Bank Street and turned left on Church Street and then back left on Canal Street. As soon as they turned onto Canal they could see flashing lights at the park across the river. They came to a halt at the crosswalk and waited for the traffic signal to change.

Abbie and Sarah became very nervous at the sight of all these lights. They could see police cars and fire and rescue units by the banks of the river. Never in Abbie's wildest imagination did she think that Brian's disappearance would lead to this. The light changed and they proceeded across the busy highway to Riverside Park.

There were policemen and rescue personnel every-where. Abbie saw a man and woman standing with her friend, Sergeant Jane Galloway. She assumed that they were Brian's parents, though she had never met them. She wanted to go over to them and say she was sorry, but wondered if those words have any meaning for them or any comfort. Abbie waited until Jane stepped away from them and then Abbie approached her.

"Hey, Jane," Abbie said quietly. Jane didn't respond. She just looked out over the river. Abbie was scared to ask, but she had to know. "Have they found him?"

Jane shook her head and wiped a tear from her cheek. "No." She hesitated for a moment and both of them looked down at the river. "We found his bicycle down there by the pier," she pointed to the posts and crossbeams holding up the pier. We were lucky it got hung up down there or we would have probably never found it. The best we can figure is that he...the bike went off the river bridge somewhere on the far side...closest to..."

Jane's voice broke, but Abbie knew what she meant. The river bridge connected Albany to the neighboring county and Brian's bike had been closer to that side when it went off the bridge.

"Any way to tell when it happened?" Abbie asked.

"No. We're not sure but most likely it was the other night after the Halloween party he attended," Jane explained.

"Have you seen Kirk?" Abbie asked, looking around the park.

"Yeah, he was here, but he left not too long ago,"

Jane replied. "Oh, by the way, speaking of Kirk, I told him that we got an identification on that skull."

This took Abbie by surprise. "Really?" she replied, her mind racing into a totally different direction.

"Yeah, some guy that was missing from Virginia about twenty years ago. There's a write-up in the paper about it today. You made the papers two days in a row. I think Kirk went to get the afternoon edition," Jane said.

"I'm going to have start a scrapbook of your news photos," Sarah joked.

"Very funny," Abbie answered with a little sarcasm.

Sarah made a funny face and said, "But what happened to the rest of him?"

"No telling," Jane sighed. If his body decomposed out there in the woods, animals could have dragged the remaining bones away or...well, who knows?"

Abbie's investigating mind went into high gear. "So, do you think there was foul play?"

"Abbie, you know I can't comment about an ongoing investigation like that, but..." she paused. "...off the record..." she leaned in very close to Abbie to make sure that no one else heard what she was about to say. "He was probably just some guy out hiking who had a heart attack or something."

This took the steam out of Abbie's curiosity. Jane was leading her on and now that she had let the cat out of the bag, she chuckled at Abbie's disappointment. "Is that it?"

"Well that's not very exciting?" Sarah said.

"Virginia State Police said that he could have been missing for as long as two months before it got reported. No family, no friends that anyone could find. It was the postman that brought it to the attention of the authorities. The guy's mail just kept piling up."

"Well, thanks for filling me in," Abbie sighed.

"I didn't tell you anything that's not in the newspaper today. It's all public information. Nothing top secret here my little super sleuth," Jane teased.

Abbie watched Brian's parents pacing back and forth on the shore of the river. She was ready to go. She had to find Kirk and see what else he had found out. "Well, we're gonna go and find Kirk. See ya later."

Abbie and Sarah waved goodbye to Jane and started pedaling towards Abbie's neighborhood. Abbie knew that Kirk was most likely in the secret underground office. He had said in his message that he was going to do some research. However, this presented a problem. Sarah was with her and the last thing she wanted to do was reveal the office to Sarah. She quickly devised a plan to keep Sarah out of the way while she tried to find Kirk.

The girls arrived at Abbie's house fifteen minutes later. Her parents weren't home when they got there, but they had left instructions for Abbie and Sarah to order a pizza. Jonathan and Cathy were enjoying a night out with dinner and a movie. Abbie ordered the pizza and told Sarah to start looking through their movie collection for a video to watch. She figured they could eat, watch a movie and continue to scan the journal for clues.

Abbie used the excuse of taking out the trash to see if Kirk was in the secret underground office. She didn't want to be gone for too long, so she just checked out the hidden hatch to see if it was locked or unlocked. When she pulled back the black plastic, she found the padlock secured which meant that Kirk had come and gone. She took out her cell phone, checked for Kirk's number on the back and called him up. It rang and rang and rang until she finally got his voice mail.

"Hey this is Kirk. Can't take your call right now, but please leave a message after the sound of the tone." A tone rang out in her ear and Abbie left Kirk a quick message to call her. She assumed that he had either turned off his phone or he didn't have a signal.

Abbie went back into the house. Sarah had picked out three movie choices. They decided on Charlie's Angels with Drew Barrymore, one of Abbie's favorite actresses. They stuck the movie into the VCR and settled into the family room for the evening. They would have the house to themselves until at least eleven o'clock or eleven-thirty.

Abbie picked up the old journal and continued reading where she left off. The pizza arrived thirty minutes later and both girls were now famished. Before long, they had devoured an entire large pizza and were feeling as stuffed as a Thanksgiving turkey.

The girls relaxed and watched the movie. Occasionally, Abbie read another entry in the journal in between her favorite scenes. Nothing she read seemed important or insightful to the case.

"Boy, I wish I could do karate like that," Sarah pointed out as they watched one of the action scenes in the movie.

Chapter Sixteen

Abbie thought back to Becca's swift moves when they ran into the ducknappers at the Peabody Hotel. She had never pegged Becca to be the type who would study karate, but after witnessing Becca in action, she realized that she too needed to add karate to her list of things to do. Maybe she would sign-up for some classes in the winter, when things slowed down a bit and she was more settled into school.

The girls finished the movie and started another one. They were halfway through Where the Heart Is starring Abbie's other favorite actress, Natalie Portman, when she noticed the clock. It was after ten o'clock and her eyelids were getting heavy.

Abbie wasn't finding anything interesting in the old journal and was about to give up hope when suddenly a few words jumped out at her. "Hey, Sarah. I think I found something."

Sarah moved from the recliner over to the couch where Abbie was sitting. "What?"

"Remember the other night at Meredith's party when her dad told us that story about the old house," Abbie began.

"Yeah, what about it?" Sarah questioned.

"Listen to this. It's one of Mr. Sullivan's last entries," Abbie smiled as she began reading from the old journal. "Today I interviewed a Josiah Aldridge, a man in his early nineties, who told me that a possible hiding place for the gold was in one of the old underground tunnels. He said that mining tunnels ran underground from the river to the old Robinson house, to the Old Bank and extended to the hills where mining camps were set-up. He drew me a map today and I'm locking it in the safe.' "

"Wow, that's a good clue," Sarah said excitedly. "But I didn't see a safe down there, did you?"

"Uh, uh," Abbie replied, biting her bottom lip. "Maybe we weren't supposed to see it. Know what I mean?"

Sarah's eyes widened. "You mean like it was hidden somewhere?"

"That's exactly what I mean," Abbie said.

Sarah peered into the book. "Is there anything else?"

"Just two more," Abbie said as she flipped the pages back and forth. " 'I have confirmed Josiah Aldridge's story about the tunnels. According to information I found today at the county archives, the tunnels were abandoned at the turn of the century. Tunnel entrances have been sealed due to the instability of the old tunnel system.' "

Sarah looked puzzled. "If they're sealed, then no one's been down there for over a hundred years," Sarah said as her face brightened. "Maybe it's down there and that's why no one's found it!"

"Sarah," Abbie sighed. "If Mr. Sullivan found this information, so have a lot of people I'm sure. Plus, just because the tunnels are sealed, doesn't mean that people haven't gone down there. They're just not open to public. Know what I mean?"

"Yeah," Sarah shrugged in disappointment. "So, what do we do next?"

Abbie's face had a blank expression. "I'm not sure. The entrance at the Old State Bank has been obviously sealed since Mr. Strickland didn't find anything."

Chapter Sixteen

"But how do we know he didn't find anything?" Sarah asked. "Maybe he's hiding it from everyone. Remember what you said the day we were there? You said yourself that he wasn't telling us the whole truth!"

"I know," Abbie replied, "but..." Abbie's cell phone rang. She recognized the caller ID as Kirk's number.

Chapter Seventeen

Abbie picked up her cell phone and pushed the receive button. Immediately, she heard static. She knew it was Kirk's voice but she could only understand a word or two here and there.

"Kirk, I can't understand you! You're breaking up? What?" Abbie repeated this over and over until finally the call was ended and Kirk was gone. She quickly picked up paper and pencil from the coffee table and jotted down the words that she understood.

"I...fell...believe...him," Abbie said out loud over and over.

"What does it mean?" Sarah asked.

Abbie looked at her blankly. "I'm not sure, but I think that Kirk's in trouble."

Again a phone rang. This time it wasn't the cell phone, but the regular phone. Its ring startled both of the girls.

Chapter Seventeen

It was almost eleven o'clock. Abbie picked up the phone and her stomach fell the moment she heard the voice on the other end.

It was Kirk's mother. "Abbie, this is Mrs. Simpson. Is Kirk over there?"

Abbie stopped breathing for a second. She was stunned. Somehow she had known that it was going to be Kirk's mom and what she was going to ask. Abbie caught her breath then said, "No, ma'am. He's not here."

There was a moment of silence on the other end that seemed to last for an eternity. "Do you know where he might be?"

"Uh...no, I'm not sure. Well, I mean he left me a message earlier today, and I think he was out looking for Brian," Abbie explained. "But I haven't seen him all day."

"He's not home yet and it's...it's late. This is not like him...to not call." Her voice was cracking up. She was nervous and scared and this sent a sickening feeling through Abbie. His mom was right. Kirk was probably one of the most responsible kids in the world. For him not to have called home meant... well, Abbie didn't want to think about what it meant.

"Do you want me to call around?" Abbie asked. She wanted to tell his mother about the broken message she had received earlier. So, why wasn't she telling her? Why couldn't she just open her mouth and say it?

"That would be great, Abbie," Mrs. Simpson replied.

They said goodbye and Abbie slowly hung up the receiver. Her assumption about Kirk being in trouble was right on target. There was the possibility that Kirk was in the secret underground office, but then again, if he was, why didn't he knock on the door? Abbie knew one thing for sure. Kirk said in an earlier message that he was going to the secret underground office, though he had not said it in so many words, probably for fear that Sarah might hear. Maybe there was a clue down there.

She looked up at Sarah who was staring at her. She was waiting for Abbie to say something. Abbie had to get to the underground office, and unfortunately she had no other choice but to divulge its secret to Sarah.

"Sarah, come with me," Abbie instructed and she got up from the couch. As they walked outside, Abbie punched in Kirk's cell phone number and tried to call him back. Maybe he had a better signal by now. The phone rang and rang. Nothing. Kirk's voice mail clicked on and Abbie left a message about his mom calling and how she was worried about him. Maybe when his signal got stronger he would get the message and somehow they would be able to connect. At least, this is what Abbie kept repeating to make herself feel better and in control. Her instincts told her that something was horribly wrong and Kirk needed her help more than ever.

The girls reached the greenhouse, which was bathed in moonlight. From the look on Sarah's face, Abbie could tell that she was totally perplexed. To Abbie's surprise, Sarah wasn't asking questions. Abbie opened the door to the greenhouse and took out her keys. Using the small flashlight on her key chain so lit up the floor of the greenhouse. Abbie pulled back the black plastic and unlocked the hatch. Before she opened it, she looked up to Sarah.

"Sarah," she began. "What I'm about to show you has to be kept a secret. And I don't mean a secret you keep for a couple of days and then blab to the whole world or let it slip in a conversation in the hallway at school. You can never and I mean never tell another living soul about this. If you do, not only will I never speak to you again as long as we live but I will make your life as miserable as possible. Do you understand?"

The serious tone of Abbie's voice scared Sarah. She looked at her in a way that Abbie had never seen before. Sarah's eyes were wide and she gasped slightly as she spoke. "Okay, I promise."

Abbie opened the hatch and climbed down the ladder. Without saying a word, Sarah followed her. When Abbie reached the floor of the secret underground office, she turned on the lights. Sarah stood there, mouth open in awe. Abbie climbed back up the ladder and closed the hatch. When she came back down, she said, "Becca and I did this a few years ago. This is where we've been running AGS Investigations since the spring of fourth grade. Have a seat." Abbie motioned for Sarah to sit in Kirk's desk chair and Abbie bent down beside her. She continued. "I really don't have time to explain all of this to you. Kirk's in trouble... I just feel it somehow. We have to find him and I'm going to need your help."

Sarah was absolutely stunned. She didn't know what to say. A thousand questions raced through her head, but the only thing she could manage to say was, "Okay."

Abbie went into action. "Earlier today, Kirk said he

had found something. If he had, he would have come down here, so look around his desk. Look in the garbage can. Look for anything that might give us a clue as to where he could have gone."

For the next several minutes the girls worked in silence. They uncrumpled wads of paper in the garbage can and discarded them when they didn't provide any clues. Abbie looked through Kirk's notebooks that were neatly arranged on the corner of his desk. Nothing.

Sarah got on the floor and started looking for anything that might have fallen behind the desk or beside it. As she was getting up, she noticed that the green power light on Kirk's computer tower, which was underneath the desk, was shining brightly in the darkness. Sarah sat up and looked at the computer monitor, which was turned off. She found the power button on the front of the monitor and pushed it.

As the screen came alive, Sarah saw what Kirk had been working on earlier that afternoon. The sound of the monitor powering up caught Abbie's attention as well and she sat down in Kirk's chair.

"Kirk must have left in a hurry. He turned off the monitor but didn't shut down the computer," Sarah deduced.

"Yeah," Abbie said as she scanned the information on the screen.

The page was like a personal log that detailed a summary of all the clues he had gathered on Brian's disappearance. Abbie read the words out loud.

"I am convinced that Brian did not run away from home. I also don't believe that he ran his bike off

147

the river bridge and drowned.

Here's what we do know:

*   Brian disappeared in the woods behind
         Meredith's house.
*   The woods back up to the wildlife refuge.
*   Brian's monster mask was found deep
         in the woods as if he had thrown it down.
*   Brian's bike was missing from Meredith's
         house, so we all thought he left.
*   His bike was found by the pier 2 days later.
*   No one at the bus station or along the
         highways have seen Brian.
*   He didn't leave a note and he hasn't
         called his parents or his aunt in Chicago
         according to his mother.

It makes sense to me that Brian never left the
woods, I think that he..."

"I think that he...what?" Abbie wondered.

"What was he going to say?" Sarah asked.

"I don't know, maybe he...." Abbie stopped. Something at the bottom of the computer screen caught her attention. This was not the only program that Kirk had open. His internet service was still up.

"Wait a minute," she said as she moved the mouse to the bottom of the screen. She clicked on the internet bar and a new image appeared on the screen. Kirk's computer was still logged on to the internet! Thank heavens for DSL, she thought to herself.

It was an archive of a Virginia newspaper article. Abbie quickly scanned it. The answers were starting to click in her head. She hit the "back" button to see what else Kirk had been researching. It was another archive newspaper article from the Albany newspaper. When Abbie saw the headline, "Maze Of Tunnels To Be Sealed," she gasped. A chill ran over her and she quickly looked up at Sarah. "Oh my gosh! That's it!"

"What's it?" Sarah pleaded.

"Come on. I'll tell you as we go," Abbie answered sharply.

"Go where?" Sarah asked again.

"We're going back to the old Palace Drug Store," Abbie explained.

Sarah's eyes grew as big as old silver dollars. "What! Abbie, it's late. Your parents will be home any minute. We can't run off in the middle of the night and–"

Abbie raised her hand to stop Sarah's babbling. "Shh! If you don't want to come with me, you can go home. But, if you really want to be a part of this detective agency you're gonna have to have some backbone and take some chances."

Sarah stopped ranting and raving. She was taken aback by Abbie's statement and merely replied, "Okay...but your parents–"

"I'll take care of that. Come on," Abbie replied as she snatched up her AGS Investigations backpack. The girls scampered up the ladder and Abbie secured the hatch behind them. When they walked around the edge of the house, Abbie breathed a sigh of relief. Her parents still weren't home, thank goodness. She and Sarah entered the house through the side door and Abbie instructed Sarah to get the copy of today's newspaper off the kitchen table. Abbie scribbled a note to her parents about going to Sarah's house to spend the night instead. She signed the note and held it up to make sure it was readable.

Abbie noticed Sarah reading the note and looking questionably at her. Abbie said, "I know...I shouldn't lie to them. But I can't very well tell them that I'm going off to save Kirk and Brian by way of a tunnel system that has been sealed for almost a century!" She placed the note where her parents would see it. Abbie snatched the newspaper from Sarah's hands and shoved it into her backpack. She ran out of the kitchen and into the family room to get the old journal. She put it in her backpack and ran back to the door.

She began to walk out of the house and realized that Sarah wasn't behind her. Abbie peered back into the house to see a stunned Sarah. "Well, are you coming?"

Sarah managed to get out two words, "Tunnel system?"

Chapter Eighteen

Sarah Martin had never pedaled her bicycle so fast in her entire life. It was all she could do to keep up with Abbie. They rode to the downtown area of Albany in record time and once again found themselves at the front door of the deserted Palace Drug Store. Both girls looked around nervously as Abbie opened the front door. Sarah felt like she was breaking and entering, even though Abbie had the key!

Abbie latched the front door behind them. She took a sleek, long flashlight out of her backpack and lit a path to the basement steps. Once they were in the stairwell she switched on the light and closed the door.

As they quickly descended the basement steps, Sarah started prodding Abbie for information. "Will you answer me already!"

"We don't have time for that, Sarah!" Abbie exclaimed.

Sarah grabbed Abbie by the shoulders and stopped

her dead in her tracks. "If you don't stop and tell me what we're doing, I can't help you!"

Abbie realized that Sarah couldn't read her mind and though all of the pieces were falling into place, Sarah was still in the dark. Abbie guided her into the office and sat Sarah down in one of the leather office chairs. "Okay, here's what I've figured out." Abbie began to pace back and forth in front of Sarah as she explained it all to her.

"Brian was out in the woods behind Meredith's house when he disappeared, right?" Abbie didn't give Sarah a chance to agree with her. "They found his Frankenstein monster mask deep in the woods, which are the same woods where the wildlife refuge begins, which are the same woods that lead up to the mountains at the edge of town. So," Abbie finally took a breath and continued. "We also know that Mr. Sullivan, Dianne's late father, discovered in his research a series of tunnels that ran from the river to the bank to other buildings downtown and out to the edge of town where there was mining going on over a hundred years ago."

"But–" Sarah tried to jump into the conversation, but Abbie kept right on going.

"Also, there was this guy in Virginia that came up missing twenty years ago and no one ever found him. Earlier this week his skull turns up in the creek bed of Crybaby Hollow, found by yours truly and my wannabe boyfriend..." Sarah perked up. "And if you ever tell anyone I just said that, I'll kill you," Abbie warned. Then she continued, "So! It's obvious!"

"What is?" Sarah asked cluelessly.

Chapter Eighteen

"Sarah. Sarah! Can't you see it! That man must have fallen out there in the woods...fallen into one of the old tunnels! Brian must have fallen out there too! And Kirk went to find him and he must have met the same fate as Brian." Abbie finished her explanation and took a small bow for Sarah.

"Hold the phone here, Abbie. There's just one problem with your little solution," Sarah pointed out. "If they have fallen into some underground tunnel and you think that the Virginia guy did the same, then how come his skull was found in the creek and not dug up or something...And hey, where is the rest of him? And why was Brian's bike found floating in the river? How did it get there?"

Abbie's smile fell. "Okay, so there are problems with my theory. But, it's the only logical explanation as to why Kirk had those two stories up on his computer and why he's now missing and left us that message is that he's in trouble. The first place we need to start looking is the tunnel system."

Sarah stood up in protest. "Now wait just a cotton pickin' minute here. Why don't we just go out to the woods and look for the place they fell in? Why don't we call your friend, the cop? Why–"

"First of all, if we can't find them from the tunnel theory, then yes, we'll go out there and look. Second of all, I want to find Kirk and Brian myself. I owe it to Kirk for not taking Brian's disappearance seriously to begin with."

Sarah nodded. "Okay, where do we start?"

"We have to find that map Mr. Sullivan made of the

tunnel system. So, look around for the safe. It has to be here somewhere," Abbie instructed as she motioned for Sarah to check behind the desk.

The girls began to search the office thoroughly. After several minutes of searching, Sarah poked her head up from behind Mr. Sullivan's desk. "Suppose we do find this safe? Any clues as to how we are going to open it?"

"We'll cross that bridge when we come to it. Keep looking," Abbie replied without giving Sarah so much as a glance.

Abbie started searching the next set of bookcases. She looked at each and every book on shelf after shelf. Suddenly, her eye caught the spine of a book near the top shelf that looked slightly different from all the rest. She reached up to pull it down, but it was either wedged too tightly or it was stuck or something. She pulled harder and this time the top of the book came loose and she heard a clicking sound from behind the bookcase. She turned to see the bookcase swing toward her.

"Bingo!" Abbie exclaimed.

Sarah raised up quickly from where she was searching under the conference table. "Wow! A secret bookcase!"

"This is way cool!" Abbie said excitedly.

Behind the bookcase was a safe with a combination lock. Sarah cast a sarcastic glance at Abbie. "Okay, we're at that bridge. How do you plan to cross it?"

"Maybe he wrote the number down somewhere in the office," Abbie suggested.

"Can you say 'needle in a haystack'?" Sarah exclaimed. "Where do you propose we start?"

"I haven't got a clue. Just look okay!" Abbie went into high gear. She started looking at other books on the bookshelf. She searched under the chairs for a written message. She looked underneath the table for any sign or clue to what the combination might be. Just when she was about to give up hope, her eyes focused on her backpack. If I was gonna hide a combination...I would hide it in my journal.

Abbie unzipped her backpack and pulled out the old journal. She flipped through the pages looking for a series of numbers that would unlock the safe. Abbie got to the end of the journal and...nothing.

"Did you find something?" Sarah asked.

"I was sure it would be in the journal. But there's nothing in there that looks like a combination," Abbie said in disgust.

"This reminds me of when I was eight and I had this combination lock for my piggy bank. So anyway, I had to write it down so like I wouldn't forget it, but silly me, I wrote each one of the numbers down in a different place and I never could remember how they went together, so I–"

Abbie held her hand up to stop Sarah from talking. "That's it, Sarah."

"Well you don't have to be so rude, I was just trying to–"

"No, I meant that's what Mr. Sullivan did! I was looking for three numbers all together, but he did the same thing you did, he wrote them down separately! Look, there's a 7 in the upper right hand corner of the inside cover and... here's a 32 in the middle of the journal and there's a 21 on the back cover!"

Chapter Eighteen

Abbie quickly went to the safe and dialed in the combination. As she turned the dial to 21, she held her breath and twisted the handle. The door to the small safe opened and Abbie reached in to pull out its contents. There were three file folders and some other small envelopes, but in the middle of the whole lot Abbie saw what she was looking for - a folded piece of paper with rough edges.

Abbie put everything back in the safe except for the map. She took it to the conference table and unfolded it. Just as the journal had described, the map detailed the tunnel system starting at the Robinson house. Abbie traced the different tunnels with her finger and found the one that led to the woods. The original tunnel started at the river and ran straight to the bank, but it also connected at the old Robinson house.

"Okay, that's it. That's where we have to go, the old Robinson house," Abbie proclaimed as she gathered up stuff. She stuffed the journal in her backpack and headed for the door.

"Hang on a second!" Sarah said, stopping her at the door. "The old Robinson house hasn't existed for years!"

"Yeah, but the foundation is still there. Come on!" Abbie pulled Sarah out of there as fast as she could.

Chapter Nineteen

The old Robinson house was only a short ride from downtown Albany. The house once stood on the south bank of the Tennessee River. It had been a very large antebellum home with tall columns and dozens of rooms.

Abbie and Sarah stood at the entrance gates to the old home. One half of the front gate was missing and the other, rusted and covered with vines, hung loosely from its hinges. As the girls looked ahead they could see a large open space where the house used to be. Pieces of the old stone steps were still present but they lead nowhere. The old perimeter of the house was covered with wild undergrowth. Abbie and Sarah walked along what used to be the front walk towards the steps.

"Abbie, do you really think this is a good idea?" Sarah asked with a little shake in her voice.

"All roads lead to this point, Sarah. If we're gonna

find Kirk and Brian, then we have to go through with this," Abbie reminded her as they approached the edge of the ruins.

Abbie shined her flashlight into the giant hole where the house had been. What used to be the basement was now covered with vines and the same undergrowth that had taken over the grounds. The beam of Abbie's flashlight caught a fallen pile of rocks. Here was their way down.

The girls walked over to the pile of rocks and carefully climbed down them to the bottom of the foundation. Abbie instructed Sarah to pull back the brush and weeds to look for any sign of a tunnel or entrance to a tunnel.

As Sarah was moving a piece of an old tree trunk, Abbie heard her screech. "What's wrong?"

"I broke a nail!" Sarah whined.

"Well bite it off and keep working," Abbie insisted without the least bit of concern for Sarah's nails.

"Bite my nail? Bite my nails!" Sarah was furious. "I have you know Abbie Walker that I have not chewed my nails since I was four...maybe five! I'm not about to bite off–"

"Fine! Then I'll do it for you!" Abbie quickly started walking over to Sarah.

Sarah swiftly put her hand behind her back. "No!" she exclaimed, holding up the other hand to stop her. "I'll clip it later."

Abbie let it go and went back to pulling weeds and moving debris. Sarah also went back to work on clearing the brush. The girls searched everywhere for any sign of a tunnel or entrance, but there was nothing.

Chapter Nineteen

"I don't understand it," Abbie said with frustration. "It has to be here...unless..." A thought was coming to her.

"Unless what?" Sarah asked.

"Unless we're not down far enough," Abbie replied.

"I don't like the sound of that," said Sarah.

Abbie shined her flashlight over the ground. "It has to be here!"

Sarah, who was cold, frustrated and tired, pointed her flashlight at Abbie who was on the ground pulling back the weeds. "Come on, Abbie," said Sarah dejectedly. "Let's just give up and go tell the police what you think. We're not going to find them on our own."

"Shut up and come over here. I need your help," Abbie commanded.

Sarah stepped over to where Abbie was. When Sarah pointed her flashlight at the ground, she saw what Abbie had found. Underneath the weeds and dirt was a hatch, very similar to the one that concealed her secret underground office.

The wooden door was about three feet square and had a rusty old handle on the corners of one end. "It's stuck," Abbie said. "Grab the other handle and help me pull!"

Abbie and Sarah pulled with all their might until the door moved slightly. "It's working! Pull harder!" Abbie yelled as she used every last bit of strength she had.

The door released suddenly accompanied by a quick rush of stale air, which sent Abbie and Sarah tumbling backwards to the ground. Without wasting a second, Abbie quickly crawled over to the open hole in front of her. Just as she stuck her flashlight into the darkness of the hole, she saw something all too familiar. A wooden ladder became visible, and then the beam of her flashlight found the dirt floor below.

"This is just like the office entrance!" Sarah exclaimed.

"Yeah, I feel right at home. Hope they are as tidy as me," she chuckled nervously, as she started to lower herself into the hole.

Just as Abbie was waist deep in the darkness, she saw that Sarah had a look of retreat on her face. Abbie glared at her and without saying a word, Sarah nodded that she would follow Abbie down the ladder.

When Abbie's feet touched the dirt floor, she let go of the ladder and started looking around the darkness with her flashlight. There was a musty smell that reminded Abbie of her grandfather's shed on the farm. As she turned in a circle surveying the room, she found what she was looking for. On one wall was another wooden door with a piece of wood nailed across it.

"I'm glad they went to a lot of trouble to seal this up, aren't you?" Abbie said sarcastically.

Sarah only whimpered in agreement as the girls crossed over to the door. The piece of wood that had been nailed across the door was fairly loose, but she needed something to pry it off. She scanned the ground around her and found a small board, which she used to pry off the barrier. The door then opened easily and ahead of them was nothing but blackness.

"You know, Abbie. This is the time in all the scary

movies where the audience says, 'no! Don't go in there!' and of course the people do and that's when something very big and hairy and icky jumps out and eats them up and–"

"Sarah!" Abbie yelled, grabbing her by the arm. "I'm scared too. But you don't have to say all that stuff and make it worse." Abbie took out the map from her backpack and shined her flashlight on it.

She quickly deduced that they needed to walk straight ahead until they came to an intersection. At that point they needed to go left, which would take them along the river toward Crybaby Hollow.

With Sarah holding on to Abbie's arm, the girls carefully proceeded down the tunnel shaft. Several minutes later they reached the intersection. Abbie pulled Sarah towards the left.

"Where do the other tunnels go?" Sarah asked as they kept walking.

"One connects to the Old State Bank and the river tunnel and the other one just goes off by itself. It wasn't labeled on the map," Abbie explained.

The girls walked further and further down the tunnel. Even Abbie was starting to wonder if they would ever get there. In her mind, she knew it would be a long hike. After all, Meredith's house was past the old section of Albany where Abbie lived. She didn't want to admit to Sarah that the distance was at least five miles in the car. By tunnel, it would probably be quicker, but Abbie wasn't sure.

After what seemed like an eternity of walking, Abbie

stopped. Sarah was starting to lag behind and she realized that they both needed a rest.

"How much further?" Sarah asked breathlessly.

"Shouldn't be much longer now," Abbie replied as she wiped the sweat from her face with her shirttail.

"Well, I'm glad of one thing," Sarah laughed.

"What's that?" Abbie asked curious of why Sarah was smiling.

"What scared me the most about coming down here was all those bodies that were buried during the civil war," Sarah continued. "You remember...the story that Meredith's dad told us around the bonfire the other night."

Abbie did remember. Now that Sarah mentioned it maybe the story that Meredith's dad told was wrong. Maybe there were no bodies buried under the old Robinson house. Maybe they had all been removed...or maybe they were buried under the dirt floor...

Abbie realized that she didn't have time to wonder about another mystery. She had to keep going. She motioned for Sarah to follow and they started down the tunnel once again. After another ten minutes of walking they came to a "Y" intersection.

Both girls stood at the entrance to the two tunnels. "Now which way?" Sarah asked.

"Good question," Abbie replied as she aimed her flashlight down the left tunnel and then peered into the darkness of the right tunnel where something caught her attention. Far down the right-handed tunnel, she could see a hint of light. "There's something down there, come on."

As they got closer to the light, Abbie realized that it was coming from directly above. They squinted upwards and Sarah realized it first.

"Stars! Those are the stars!" she yelled for joy.

"Yeah, a hole. That's exactly how I think Brian disappeared," Abbie suggested.

Sarah shone her flashlight around the tunnel. "No sign of him here. Do you think he might have crawled further down the tunnel," Sarah added as she pointed the beam of light into the darkness ahead.

"No," Abbie said simply. "I have a feeling he and Kirk are both in the other tunnel. Come on."

Abbie and Sarah backtracked their way to the "Y" and took the path of the other tunnel. After walking for at least another five minutes, they came to a dead end. Directly ahead of them, their flashlights revealed nothing but rock, where part of the tunnel had obviously caved in some time ago.

"Now what?" Sarah shrugged. "There's like no way we can dig through that."

"If only we could get Kirk to answer his cell phone," Abbie wished.

Sarah sighed. "Too bad you guys don't have walkie-talkies."

The last piece of the puzzle clicked into place. She and Kirk used to have walkie-talkies but they only used them when they went out on surveillance. But now they had something better. She remembered Kirk's instructions about the cell phones and how they had a two-way radio built into them that was much more powerful than their old walkie-talkies.

Abbie pulled out her cell phone and chose the two-way radio option from the menu. Instantly, she heard the sound of Kirk's voice. "Anyone there? Abbie...please."

Abbie pressed the side talk button on the phone. "Kirk! It's me and Sarah!"

A much more energetic voice responded. "Abbie! Is that really you?"

"Yes, Kirk. It's me!" Abbie exclaimed.

"And me, too!" Sarah added with excitement.

"Kirk, we're in the tunnels and I think we're pretty close to you. There's a huge pile of rocks that's blocking us from going any further."

Kirk was breathing heavy. "Yeah. I know where you're talking about. I think we're just on the other side!"

Abbie smiled. "Does that mean you have Brian with you?"

"Yeah, but Abbie, he and I are both hurt," Kirk answered.

Abbie and Sarah's smiles fell. "How bad?" Abbie asked.

"I think Brian's shoulder is dislocated and I think I broke my leg. I put it in a splint I made with some boards I found down here and our belts. You have to get us out of here," Kirk pleaded.

"We will, Kirk. Just hang on," Abbie replied.

"What are we going to do?" Sarah asked. "It'll take forever to go back through the tunnels."

Abbie thought for a second and then grabbed Sarah's

arm, "Follow me." She counted the steps aloud as she pulled Sarah along with her.

Once Abbie had finished counting, she looked up and saw a glimmer of the night sky through the hole above. Proud of her detective work she grinned and turned back to Sarah, "I'm going to get on your shoulders and try to reach that hole above. Then, I'll lower a rope down to you and pull you up, okay?"

"You have rope in your backpack?" Sarah asked, surprised.

"A girl always has to be prepared," said Abbie, as they reached the spot they had been at before.

Abbie climbed onto Sarah's shoulders and slowly steadied herself as she reached for the opening above her. Abbie was just tall enough to get her arms through the hole and pull herself up and out of the tunnel. Abbie looked around and realized that she was in the woods behind Meredith's house. She recognized Meredith's blue porch lights in the distance.

Working quickly, she opened her backpack and took out the rope. She tied a loop in one end of the rope big enough for Sarah's foot and lowered it into the darkness. "Put one foot in the loop and hold on to the rope, Sarah."

Abbie stepped back from the hole and wrapped the rope around the closest tree for leverage. She took a firm grip on the rope and started pulling as hard as she could. She pulled and pulled until the upper part of Sarah's body began to emerge from the hole. Sarah struggled to pull herself up, and Abbie, keeping a firm grip on the tension of the rope, inched her way towards Sarah. When she was within grasp, Abbie took hold of Sarah's wrists and pulled her out of the hole.

"Thanks," Sarah said breathlessly. "That was a little scary."

"I've been in worse spots," Abbie sighed. "Come on." Abbie checked her map, got her bearings and started tracing the path to where Kirk should be.

"What are you doing?" Sarah asked, following behind Abbie.

"I counted the number of steps it took to get from the caved in part of the tunnel to that opening back there," Abbie stopped. "The place where Kirk fell, should be around here somewhere." She took out her cell phone and hit the two-way radio button. "Kirk. Come in, Kirk."

"I'm here. Where are you?" Kirk asked.

"I should be close to where you are. Yell, so we can hear you," she instructed.

"Okay, but it won't do much good. We've been yelling down here forever. It's a long way up," Kirk told her.

"Yell anyway!" Abbie exclaimed. "Sarah, get down on your hands and knees and start crawling around. Get as close to the ground as you can and listen for Kirk!"

Sarah didn't like the idea of crawling on the ground, but she didn't argue with Abbie. Both girls got on their hands and knees and started combing every square inch of ground in the vicinity of where Kirk should be. The leaf-covered terrain was moist from the night dew.

Suddenly, Abbie stopped. Faintly, she could hear

the sound of someone singing. "Sarah, do you hear that?"

Sarah also stopped and held her breath, trying desperately to hear what Abbie was hearing. "It sounds like someone is singing...singing the national anthem."

The girls began crawling faster towards the sound of Kirk's singing until it got stronger and stronger. To her left she caught a glimpse out of the corner of her eye of Sarah starting to sink into the earth. She heard Sarah's scream and Abbie hurled herself onto Sarah's feet. Before Sarah could disappear into the hole, Abbie stopped her from falling. Moving deliberately, Abbie pulled Sarah back out of the hole.

"I don't think you want to go down there," Abbie joked as she carefully approached the edge of the hole.

"That's the second time you've saved me," Sarah said in relief.

"Yeah, I'm keeping track for future reference," Abbie said as she stuck her flashlight into the hole. Far below she could see Kirk and Brian lying on the ground. The distance to the bottom of this tunnel was much further than the one she and Sarah had maneuvered.

"How are you making it?" Abbie yelled down to Kirk and Brian.

"We'll be better once we're out of here!" Kirk exclaimed.

"Brian, I know a bunch of people who are going to be glad to see you," Abbie said almost giggly with relief to see him.

"Good! Maybe they'll feed us. Actually we thought

you might be the pizza delivery guy. We're starving!" Brian joked as he rubbed his shoulder.

Abbie took the rope and started lowering it down to them. As it came within Kirk's grasp he yelled back up to her, "I hope you don't expect either one of us to climb this thing."

"Oh," Abbie realized that with their injuries there was no way they could manage. "I forgot. Hang on!"

"We're not going anywhere, that's for sure," Brian said sarcastically.

Abbie turned to Sarah. "Sarah, run to Meredith's house and call 911."

"Why don't you just call them on your cell phone?" Sarah asked.

"Look," Abbie pointed at the face of her cell phone. "No signal. The only thing working out here is the two-way radio system. Hurry, Sarah."

Sarah nodded, "On my way!"

Abbie pointed her in the right direction. She turned back to the boys. "Okay, I just sent Sarah for help."

"Hey! Pull your rope up. I've attached a little surprise for you!" Kirk exclaimed.

Abbie pulled on the rope until a tattered briefcase came into view. Using her flashlight, she examined it. "What is it?"

"A briefcase you dummy," Kirk replied.

"Well, I know that. What's in it?" Abbie asked.

From behind, Abbie heard a strangely familiar voice. "Nothing that concerns you, Abbie Walker. Step aside."

Chapter Twenty

Before Abbie turned around, a rush of memories went through her head. This voice was the missing key to a haunting puzzle. As she turned, she saw the shadowy figure of a girl about her height with long hair. When Abbie's flashlight stopped on the girl's face, the final piece of the puzzle fell in place.

"Chloe," Abbie said slowly.

"Ah, you remember me. I'm honored," Chloe said smugly.

The ongoing nightmare of being chased, the girl's voice in her dream...these images were all crystal clear now. All of it had not been a dream, but something very real from her past.

"It's been a long time, hasn't it?" Chloe asked as she tossed her hair out of her face.

"Apparently, not long enough," Abbie replied. "I've

had dreams–dreams about us riding bikes and being chased and being...in these woods. Why can't I remember anymore?"

"Because you weren't supposed to remember anything," Chloe explained. "Three years ago, we met on the front steps of your house. I gave you a necklace that was actually a stolen artifact with some pretty amazing powers. The Group wanted it back, but my people wanted it more. And yes...we were being chased. Not too far from here, actually. Isn't it funny that we should both end up here again, just three short years later?"

"Yeah, it's real funny," said Abbie evenly. She looked down at the tattered old briefcase and then back up to Chloe. "So, what's in here?"

"Ah, well that's really none of your concern. But I do appreciate you and your little sidekick finding it," Chloe said as she looked down into the hole. "Hello, Kirk. Been a long time."

Abbie could hear Kirk and Brian talking down below but she couldn't make out what they were saying. She picked up the briefcase and held it close.

"I want to know what's in here," Abbie demanded.

"Abbie!" Kirk shouted. "What's going on up there? Who is that?"

Abbie ignored him. She kept her eyes focused on the girl standing in front of her, watching her every move.

Chloe let out a sound of disgust and shook her head. "Abbie, you don't want to get involved. This is way out of your league."

"I'll take my chances," Abbie replied firmly.

"Agents in my...organization...saw the news article about the missing skull you found. As you know, it was a man from Virginia who worked for the NSO, National Security Organization, which is better known in my circles as 'The Group.' Anyway, twenty years ago, he was on the run and for some unknown reason, he ended up here in Albany, Alabama. He was carrying that briefcase, which contains longitudes and latitudes of every nuclear launch site in the world."

Abbie was stunned. Chloe's story was like something off of television. Whether it was true or not, she knew that giving Chloe the briefcase was a very bad idea. Just as she was about to tell her this, the sound of distant sirens became clearer and clearer.

"Okay, I've told you. Now come on. Give it to me!" Chloe exclaimed.

Abbie looked down at the hole in the ground. She could throw the briefcase back down to Kirk where Chloe couldn't get to it so easily. Just as Abbie was about to toss the suitcase, something in her gut told her to take the briefcase and run - run to the old wooden bridge at Crybaby Hollow. She tightened her grip on the briefcase and snapped back at Chloe, "No!" With that, she turned and started running. Without giving a thought to her own safety, she knew that she had to get as far away from Chloe as possible. Instinctively, she dodged large trees, saplings and logs on the ground to sprint away from capture. From the sounds she heard behind her, Chloe was in pursuit. There was no time to think, Abbie just had to run!

Chapter Twenty

Using the moonlight and her flashlight as a guide, Abbie managed to stay ahead of Chloe. Branches beat at her. One scratched her face, but nothing was going to stop her! She was determined to get away...far away.

Chloe had not expected Abbie to run, nor would she have guessed that Abbie would be able to run as fast as she did. Chloe had only gone a short distance when she tripped over a rock and fell to the ground, giving Abbie the chance to get further away from her.

Abbie, realizing that Chloe was not right on her heels, stopped briefly to get her bearings. She looked in all directions, searching for anything familiar. Suddenly, she heard the sound of water and then something caught her eye. To her right, she could see the bridge! Crybaby Hollow and the bridge were just ahead.

Abbie ran in the direction of the bridge. She remembered that there was a place under the bridge that she could hide. From there she could use her cell phone to call for help. Tyler's cell phone had had a signal there and surely hers would too!

Abbie reached the edge of the woods where the road began. She slid down the incline and landed near one end of the bridge. Just as she stepped on the old wooden bridge, headlights flashed on her from the other side of the bridge. From behind her, she heard the approach of another car and its headlights blinded her as she turned around. The car stopped at the edge of the bridge, it's engine still running. Stalemate.

Now what? Abbie thought to herself. She had to take

a chance. She slowly approached the first car, hoping that it would be Jane or another policeman or even a park ranger.

The car door opened and Abbie could see the figure of a young woman stepping out onto the bridge. Abbie had no idea why she knew, but she knew that this was another person from her past...a good person that was here to help. Abbie looked back to the woods. She sensed that Chloe was getting closer and closer to the bridge. Taking a chance, Abbie moved closer to the woman standing by the car.

As she approached her, Abbie saw another face from her dreams. She recognized her, but couldn't remember her name. "I know you...you were here. Just like this...with the car and the headlights and it was dark just like this and I was on my bike and..."

The young woman came closer to Abbie and put her hand on her shoulder. "Abbie, it's okay. I'm Natty. And yes, we've been here together before. How do you remember that? Did Chloe tell you?"

"I've been dreaming about it," Abbie answered. At that moment, Chloe came out of the woods and stepped onto the bridge.

The young woman and Chloe stared at each other intensely. Abbie could tell they were not exactly happy to see each other. Natty let go of Abbie and walked in front of her, blocking Abbie from Chloe.

"Chloe. It's been a long time–" she began.

"I don't want any trouble, Natty," Chloe said.

"Neither do I," Natty replied.

"I just want the briefcase."

Natty laughed. "I don't think so, Chloe. You go back to Jack and tell him that I said to crawl back in the hole he came from and leave this girl alone."

Chloe smirked, "He doesn't want her. He wants the briefcase. It's worth–"

"I know what it's worth. And, it's never going to pay off for him. It's going back to Washington where it belongs," said Natty.

"We'll just see about that," Chloe said, raising her arm into the air. When she did this, headlights flipped on down the road on the other side of the bridge.

Natty barely flinched. She walked closer to Chloe until she was just inches away from her and whispered, "Go tell Jack that he doesn't want a war with us. But, if he does, we're ready." She tapped a button on the side of her wristwatch. From out of the woods, several people sprang with rifles aimed.

Startled, Abbie retreated until she hit the hood of the car. She watched as Chloe quickly stepped backwards away from Natty. Without saying a word, Chloe cast an evil look at Natty and then turned and ran towards the waiting car. Natty stayed absolutely still until Chloe got in the car and it turned around and drove away into the night.

When all was clear, Natty raised her wristwatch to her mouth, pushed a button and said, "All clear. Tango team, they are leaving the area heading due east on county road 342. Pursue and attempt to intercept. Alpha team, Miss Walker and I are going for a walk. Secure the perimeter and wait for my instructions."

Chapter Twenty

The armed figures withdrew and scattered back into the woods. Natty turned around to see a wide-eyed Abbie. "May I?" she asked as she held her hands out for the briefcase.

Abbie handed it to her and Natty put it in the car. She locked the car with her remote and then approached Abbie again. "Let's go for a walk. We need to talk."

Chapter Twenty-One

Abbie and Natty walked back into the woods towards the spot where Kirk and Brian were trapped. As they got closer to the area, Abbie could see lots of people and the emergency lights flashing. The fire and rescue department had set up portable work lights in the woods to make the rescue easier.

When they reached the site, Natty walked ahead instructing Abbie to stay back. Abbie watched Natty flash her credentials to the officers-in-charge. She then turned and motioned for Abbie to come over. When Abbie reached the group of adults, she recognized a familiar face.

"Why am I not surprised to find you here, young lady?" Sergeant Jane Galloway asked.

"I guess I just have a knack of being the in the right place at the right time," Abbie replied.

"Uh huh," Jane said shaking her head.

"Are Kirk and Brian going to be all right?" Abbie asked.

"They're a little worse for wear, but yeah, they're gonna be fine," Jane assured her. "Brian's in the ambulance over there and the rescue team is about to lift Kirk out of the hole."

"Good," Abbie said in relief. "Oh, Natty, this is my friend, Jane Galloway."

Natty smiled. "Actually, we kind of know each other, Abbie. My older sister was friends with Jane in college."

"Small world, huh?" Jane asked, smiling at Abbie.

"So that's how you've kept up with me and–"

Natty stopped her by pulling her away. When they were out of earshot, she said, "Yes, that's one of the ways we've kept up with you, Abbie. Let's see about Kirk and then... well, then we need to talk."

Abbie understood. The rescue team had just hoisted Kirk out of the hole and now they were placing him on a stretcher. Abbie and Natty walked over to him.

"Abbie!" Kirk exclaimed. "Who was that Chloe girl and–"

Abbie quickly put her finger to her mouth to signal Kirk to shut up. Then, she whispered, "I'll tell you later. Just take it easy, okay?"

"I will," Kirk said in relief. "Abbie? Thanks for coming for me and Brian."

"No problem," Abbie smiled.

The paramedics were about to roll Kirk away, when he stopped them and called back to Abbie. "Oh! I almost forgot. There's something down there you need to see."

Chapter Twenty-One

Abbie cast an inquisitive look back to him. "What?"

"Let's just say that we may have solved two mysteries tonight," Kirk replied. The paramedics wheeled him away, but Abbie didn't need any further explanation.

She turned to Natty. "I need to go down there."

Natty looked at her, but oddly didn't question her reasoning. Natty stepped over to the man operating the hoist and flashed her credentials again. He motioned for some other men to stop what they were doing. There was a small cage, just big enough to hold Natty and Abbie, attached to the large steel hook. The crew was just getting ready to go back down for the rest of their rescue equipment, but stopped to let Natty take Abbie down into the hole. Abbie and Natty got into the cage and the crane operator lowered the basket back into the hole.

As they were being lowered, Abbie couldn't believe how far down it actually was. When they reached the bottom, the rescue lights revealed a much wider tunnel than the other tunnels Abbie had seen. On one side of the tunnel was an underground stream that came out of a smaller hole several feet away from them. Obviously, the water was from the river and Abbie deduced that from the direction the tunnel was heading, this must be the stream that eventually flowed under the bridge at Crybaby Hollow. The skull must have worked its way out of the tunnel to the stream.

"Okay, so what do you need to see down here?" Natty asked, looking around.

"Well, Kirk said that we solved two mysteries tonight," she explained. "Of course the first is that we found Brian.

As far as mysteries go, I think we actually solved three. The skull Tyler and I found in Crybaby Hollow had to have originated down here. Kirk found the man's briefcase, so I'm sure if we look around, we'll find the rest of him...or what's left of him at least."

"And the third?" Natty inquired.

Abbie stepped further down the tunnel until she practically tripped over what she was looking for. In the shadows of the rescue lights, Abbie found a steel box the size of a footlocker. Natty moved one of the lights so they could see the box more clearly.

Fragments of an old lock were lying on the ground. Obviously, Kirk had knocked it off with a rock. Abbie unclasped the latch and opened the lid. Inside, she discovered stacks and stacks of Confederate bills of all denominations. The missing gold wasn't gold at all. It was Confederate money!

"Oh my," Natty said in disbelief.

"Well, that figures," Abbie said in a disgusted voice.

"What do you mean?" Natty asked.

"Whenever you go searching for pots of gold at the end of the rainbow, you come up empty," she explained. "A bunch of worthless Confederate money."

Natty's eyebrows rose. "Not worthless, Abbie. To collectors the bills that are in good condition are worth a lot."

"Really?" Abbie's face brightened.

"Abbie, we need to talk and I don't have much time," Natty explained. She motioned for her to take a seat on the ground and then Natty sat on top of the box.

"I work for an organization called the National

Security Organization. However, most people call it 'The Group' because it was formed by a group of men over fifty years ago. These men worked for the government and when they retired or left the agencies they worked for, they formed the NSO to do things that government agencies couldn't do."

Abbie's eyes widened. From what she had seen tonight, Abbie knew Natty was important, but had no idea that she was top secret!

"One of their projects was to identify young people with special gifts. They trained them, paid for their college and in return the young people had to give a few years of service to the NSO. After that, some stayed with NSO, some went to the CIA or FBI or Secret Service...well, you get the picture. In the mid-seventies, Jack, one of the founding members double-crossed the others and turned against the US government and the NSO. We, the NSO, call them the Shadow People because, well...to be honest, you never know when one of their operatives is around. They blend. They... well, they do horrible things."

Abbie cringed. Natty's explanation was like something out of a James Bond film.

"Twenty years ago, Walter Carson, who worked for us, left Virginia with the top-secret documents in that briefcase you and Kirk recovered. The NSO lost communications with him two days after he left Virginia. He was supposed to meet up with another agent, but he never made it. The NSO traced him as far as Albany."

Abbie interrupted her. "But what does this have to

do with me?"

"Nothing...really," Natty replied. "At least not until three years ago. Chloe was one of our most promising students at the academy. But she turned and stole a highly top secret artifact we called the Timepiece. She ended up here in Albany. We think she was trying to help the shadow people find the briefcase by using the Timepiece. But, something went wrong in her plan. That's where you came into the picture."

"But how would Chloe know me?" Abbie asked with a look of confusion.

"That's where things get a little sticky. Chloe had learned that you were on a list of candidates for the academy. Originally, you were turned down, but for some reason, Chloe wanted to make sure you got back on the list. Honestly, we don't know why she has singled you out as an adversary. Maybe someday we will."

"I was turned down?" Abbie asked dejectedly. "Why?"

"Oh, don't feel bad. Lots of kids are put on the list based on state testing scores and well, I really can't tell you exactly how we identify them, but lots of kids are crossed off too. Now, the good thing is that after your little episode with the Timepiece three years ago, you were put back on the list and assigned to me."

"But I don't really remember what happened with Chloe. I just remember..."

Natty held her hand up to stop her from going on. "I can't explain this to you right now. You were not supposed to remember any of it. For you, it should have never happened. But, for some reason, we just couldn't wipe all of it out of your memory. That's why you were having the dreams and the feelings of deja vu you told me about. Anyway, last summer I was in Memphis when you found those ducks from the Peabody Hotel and you and your friend Becca recovered those stolen diamonds."

"You were? I don't remember seeing you there. I just remember this old man who talked to me-" Abbie suddenly had a realization. "The old man is your boss, isn't he?"

"I can't say I approved of the way he approached you to make first contact, but nevertheless, as you say, he is the boss," said Natty. "After your work in Memphis, you were placed on the top of the list. We had not planned on approaching you until summer, but when your picture ended up in the newspaper with Walter Carson's skull, we knew the shadow people wouldn't be far behind."

Natty got up and stared down at the box. "Well, I guess we had better drag this thing over to the cage and let them lift it out of here."

"Hang on a second," Abbie said, stopping her. "So, now what? Is that Chloe girl and those people gonna keep coming after me?"

Natty looked down at her and pushed Abbie's tattered hair out of her face. "You're safe, Abbie. They wanted the briefcase, not you."

"But you said Chloe wanted me for an adversary or something?" Abbie questioned.

"I don't know what Chloe's agenda is, except for not wanting you to be forgotten and believe me, no one at NSO is going to forget you," Natty assured her.

Chapter Twenty-One

Abbie sighed. "And...what's next?"

"The next thing we have to do is get out of here," Natty replied. Abbie started to interrupt her again, but Natty put her finger over Abbie's lips to quiet her. "All in due time my dear. We need to get out of here and get you home. Your parents are going to be worried."

"Oh my gosh, my parents!" Abbie exclaimed. In all of the excitement, she had forgotten that she and Sarah had just sort of left with only a vague note for her parents.

"I'm going to take care of everything, Abbie. Don't worry," Natty assured her. "Besides, your parents should be used to your high jinks by now, right?"

Abbie smiled. She helped Natty pull the box over to the cage and the rescue workers above pulled the box and the two of them out of the hole. As Abbie left the darkness of the hole behind, she couldn't help but wonder what had happened to the rest of poor old Walter Carson.

Chapter Twenty-Two

In all of the confusion, Abbie had completely forgotten about Sarah. She found her with Meredith and her parents, who by that time had called Sarah's parents who had called Abbie's parents. All of them were gathered at the closest point the police would allow them to get, waiting for Abbie and Sarah and news of Kirk and Brian.

Abbie felt her stomach turn when she saw her parents in the crowd of people. Natty stepped ahead and pulled all of the parents together. She once again flashed her credentials and spoke to them for what seemed like an eternity.

When she had finished, Abbie's parents weren't mad. Sarah's parents weren't mad. They all were just happy to see their children safe and sound.

* * *

The autumn days of November were accompanied

by turning leaves of orange and brown, which covered the ground. Life in Albany, Alabama returned to normal... except for Abbie Walker. The events of that night in the woods had forever changed her. She had answers to the haunting dream, but she was also plagued with puzzling questions about "The Group" and "the shadow people" and what was going to happen next.

Natty had not told anyone...parents, Jane or other kids– about the details surrounding the skull or the briefcase. She had released just enough information to the authorities and the parents to keep everyone satisfied. However, Abbie knew the truth. She knew there was a great deal more to the story - even more than what Natty had told her in the underground tunnel. There were still unanswered questions in her mind as to why Walter Carson came to Albany, Alabama to start with. Who was he? Did he have some connection to Albany? Or, was he meeting someone here in Albany who worked with the NSO?

Abbie pondered these questions, but she never shared one bit of the information she had learned that night with Kirk or Sarah. Kirk had not been too excited to learn that Sarah was now partner number three in AGS Investigations. He always figured that the firm would stay somewhat of a trio, with Becca involved via phone and internet. Now, there were four of them that knew about the secret underground office and the case files. He was not totally convinced that Sarah could keep their secret, but Abbie was confident about her decision to involve Sarah and Kirk wouldn't dispute it openly.

Kirk's leg had been broken, but it was only a hairline fracture. Brian's shoulder was dislocated and he ended up spending a couple of days in the hospital under observation. Kirk's leg was in a cast from his knee to the tips of his toes, which prevented him from climbing down the ladder to the underground office for about six weeks.

Sarah took her new responsibilities with AGS Investigations very seriously. In fact, Abbie was truly shocked to see this side of her. Any doubt that Abbie had about Sarah being able to keep a secret was washed away. It didn't take Abbie long to realize that Sarah was really smarter than anyone ever gave her credit for. Her "dumb" act was just that...an act. She used it to mask her true intelligence, which she perceived as a turn off to boys and a hindrance to getting in with the popular crowd.

Curious about Sarah, Abbie had Kirk do a little investigating with the Albany City School records from his computer at home. He was able to tap into a backdoor in the system and learn that Sarah had never made less than a "A" in any class since she started school.

As for Natty, she had shown up at just the right time and then had disappeared. After she settled things with the parents and the authorities, she left as quickly as she came. The last words she left with Abbie were, "I'll be in touch with you soon. There are some exciting days ahead of you." Abbie tried not to think to hard about "what" kind of exciting days were ahead.

With Christmas fast approaching, Abbie took an afternoon job with Lydia Ives at the City Museum of Art and Natural History. A few years earlier, Abbie had wanted to work for Lydia, but her parents didn't want her to work during the school year. So, she had worked on and off during the summer months helping Lydia with light office work.

The museum had been built ten years ago in an effort to create a cultural center for Albany. Following a major renovation of the Princess Theatre, the city built a beautiful museum across the street to house exhibits of art, photography and the natural history of the Tennessee River valley.

Abbie's afternoon job consisted of answering the phone, filing, running errands, preparing for special events and working on special projects. Two weeks before Christmas, a "special project" came into the museum, which Lydia assigned to Abbie since she was the one responsible for finding it.

Chapter Twenty-Three

"Busy?" Lydia asked, standing in the doorway of the workroom.

"Not too bad," Abbie replied. "I've got all of these envelopes stuffed, stamped and ready to mail out. If you want me to, I'll drop them off at the post office on my way home."

Lydia smiled and took a seat across from her. "I'll take those. I think you're going to be busy for the rest of the afternoon."

Abbie gave her a puzzled look. "Okay...what's up?"

"I've just come from a meeting about the box of Confederate money that you found," Lydia explained.

"Really?" Abbie said in a surprised tone. "I just figured that it would go back to Dianne's family, since..."

Lydia cut her off. "Dianne was one of the people I was having the meeting with," Lydia admitted. "Most of the money was still intact, and she feels that the trunk and its contents need to be here at the museum."

Chapter Twenty-Three

Abbie's face brightened. "But what about selling the Confederate individual bills and–"

"Hang on. Let me finish," Lydia injected. "The mayor feels and Dianne agrees, that her father would want the trunk placed here at the museum. The Confederate bills need to be catalogued, examined and if the committee we've formed feels that we want to sell them to a collector, we could actually do it like a silent auction and raise money for the museum."

"Oh...well, that's a great idea!" Abbie said happily. "Do you want me to help you get a mailing together about that or what...?"

Lydia didn't say a word. She was grinning from ear to ear and Abbie knew there was more to this than what she was telling. "The Mayor, Dianne and the rest of the committee want you to be the one to do the cataloguing and the set-up of the exhibit...along with my supervision and mentoring, of course."

Abbie beamed. "You're kidding me? You have to be! I mean this is great!"

Lydia jumped up from her seat to hug her young apprentice. "And I didn't even have to talk them into it. It was actually Dianne's idea. She said that with your investigating interests, this would be a great experience for you. She said, 'that young lady solved a mystery in a few days that took my Daddy all his adult life to work on.' "

"I just put the pieces together. He did all the real work," Abbie said humbly.

"Well young lady, the real work lies ahead," Lydia added.

Chapter Twenty-Three

"Is the trunk here? At the museum?" Abbie asked excitedly.

"It's downstairs in Workroom A," Lydia replied. "While I take this mailing over to the post office, why don't you go down there and start removing the contents of the trunk?"

"Really?" Abbie asked.

"Yeah," Lydia replied picking up the box of mailers. "But remember to put on the gloves and handle each bill with care. Just separate the bills by their condition, okay?"

"Not a problem," Abbie said as she headed out the door and towards the staircase. She sped down the stairs to the real working area of the museum. There were several rooms set up with worktables and equipment for the building and handling of exhibits. The trunk was in the first workroom past the stairs.

As Abbie entered the room, her eyes fell upon the old trunk. Of all the mysteries she had solved, this one brought her more joy than any of the others. It wasn't a joy for herself, but it was the joy she saw on Dianne's face after it was found. Her eyes had welled with tears and the embrace she gave Abbie for bringing closure to such an important thing in her father's life, was worth more than any amount of money.

Abbie put on the rubber gloves and carefully opened the lid of the trunk. She decided to take all of the money out of the trunk and stack it on the worktable for sorting. Abbie took her time, since many of the bills were crumbling from old age.

Just as Abbie was removing the last stack from the

bottom of the trunk, she noticed something odd about the interior lining of the bottom of the trunk. In one corner, the lining didn't meet up with the walls of the trunk. That's odd, she thought to herself. Abbie reached into the corner and carefully peeled up one edge of the lining. To her surprise, she found a false bottom to the trunk.

Placing her fingers under the edge of the false bottom, Abbie slowly pulled it up and out of the trunk. A large faded envelope was stuck to the real bottom of the trunk. Abbie assumed it was stuck to the bottom because of the many years it had been there. Using a tool, which looked like a spatula, she inserted it under the envelope in hopes that it would pull away easily. To her amazement, it did.

Abbie laid the envelope on a separate worktable. Working delicately, she opened the envelope and peered inside. What she saw inside made her gasp. There was a piece of parchment and the markings she could see were strangely familiar. It was a map and a folded piece of paper with handwriting.

Abbie set the envelope down and closed the workroom door. She had only taken a couple of steps, when she decided to go back to the door and lock it. She didn't want someone from the museum to see what she had found - at least not yet. Abbie carefully slid the document out of the envelope. The map was similar to the one that Dianne's father had drawn of the tunnel system. This map of the tunnel system, however, had much greater detail of the tunnel system.

Abbie set the map aside and opened the letter.

Chapter Twenty-Three

July, 1865

James,

I do not know if this letter will find you We are camped on the shores of the river waiting for the Yanks to leave the area. We have been safe guard ing the payroll and shipment of gold in a cave for several days. Our food and water supply are almost exhausted.

We are leaving this trunk that contains the payroll. It won't do those Yanks any good. We are carrying the gold with us to a safe location that one of our scouts has located. You are the only one who knows of this hidden compartment. Should you find this letter, it will be accompanied by a map showing the location of where we are leaving the gold.
Best of luck,
Steven Dalton

Abbie gasped. The story of the lost gold shipment was real. It was possibly still out there somewhere! Now what? She thought to herself. An idea came to her. She placed the letter and the map into a new, larger envelope and put the old envelope back where she found it in the bottom of the trunk. Abbie replaced the false bottom and closed the lid to the trunk.

She scribbled a note to Lydia and put it on her office door where she would find it. She had to hurry. The Old State Bank would be closing in fifteen minutes and she had to see Mr. Ray Strickland and she had to see him immediately.

Chapter Twenty-Four

When Abbie arrived at the Old State Bank, a young woman was sweeping the front porch of the old bank. Abbie didn't recognize her. She was in her twenties with short blonde hair and glasses.

"Can I help you?" she asked.

"Uh...I'm looking for Mr. Strickland. Is he inside?" Abbie asked.

"No, honey. He's already left for the day. I'm Shelley, his assistant. Is there anything I can do for you?"

"Not really. Are you sure Mr. Strickland is gone?" Abbie explained.

"He left about half an hour ago, but he'll be in tomorrow morning at nine a.m. Guess you'll just have to wait until then," Shelley said.

Abbie bit her bottom lip. She needed to get inside of the old bank and she wasn't sure she could wait until tomorrow. Actually it was better that Mr. Strickland wasn't there for what Abbie needed to do.

"You know, maybe you can help me," Abbie began. "I'm doing this report for school about banks of the 1800's and I would really love to see the vault. Is that possible?"

The girl stopped sweeping and pushed her glasses back up on her nose. "I don't see why not. Come on in."

Abbie followed her into the main lobby of the bank. She noticed the open vault door behind the counter where tellers once sat to conduct business. She eased her way around the counter area and casually entered the vault. Just as she stepped inside the phone rang, giving her a start.

Abbie took a deep breath and moved further inside the vault to inspect the walls. According to the lost gold legend a tunnel ran from the river to the Old State Bank and directly into this vault. Abbie meticulously searched every square inch of the walls looking for any sign of where a secret door may have once been.

Abbie was on her knees with her back to the vault's entrance and practically jumped out of her skin when Shelley spoke, "Finding everything all right?" Shelley had finished her phone conversation and entered the vault.

Startled, Abbie twirled around to look up at her. "Oh, yes, these old vaults are just fascinating aren't they?"

Shelley looked perplexed. "Uh...I suppose so. Looks like concrete walls to me. Boy, I'd hate to get locked in one of these things. Got claustrophobia. I hate places like this."

Abbie smiled. "It is kind of small, isn't it?"

"Well, I hate to run you off, but I've got to be locking up now," the young lady said as she pulled out a ring of keys.

Chapter Twenty-Four

"Oh, well...sure," Abbie replied. The phone rang again.

"Excuse me. I'll be right back," Shelley said as she went to the small office.

Abbie poked her head out of the vault, "I'll just let myself out!" Abbie couldn't see Shelley anymore.

She had disappeared into a back room, but obviously heard Abbie, because Abbie heard her yell out, "Okay, thanks for coming in!"

Abbie quickly walked to the front doors. She opened one door and slammed it shut to make Shelley think someone had walked out the door. Abbie bent down and scurried across the lobby to a back hallway. She quietly started opening doors, looking for a place to hide.

On her second try, she discovered a small closet and stepped inside. Trying not to make a sound, she closed the door behind her and crouched down in the darkness to wait. She would give Shelley ten minutes to exit the building and then she would come out of hiding.

Ten minutes seemed like forever to Abbie. After only a few minutes, she thought she heard the front door open and close, which she assumed was Shelley leaving for the day. However, Abbie decided to stay put for the full ten minutes just to be on the safe side.

After the ten minutes were up, Abbie slowly and quietly turned the doorknob and opened the closet door. She stopped and listened for any sounds of anything stirring in the building. She heard nothing and decided the coast was clear. Abbie tiptoed out of the closet and peered around the corner of the hallway entrance to make sure the lobby was indeed empty. No one was there.

Abbie turned back to the hallway and started opening doors again. This time she wasn't looking for a closet. She was looking for the door to the basement. If her assumption was correct, the entrance to the tunnel system was directly below the vault.

After checking several doors, Abbie hit pay dirt. The staircase looked just like the one that led down to the basement of the old Palace Drug Store. Abbie took out her keys and used the tiny flashlight on her key ring. Of all the times not to have my AGS backpack! That backpack was filled with the necessities of the trade.

She looked for a light switch but couldn't find one. Abbie carefully eased her way down the old wooden steps into pitch, black darkness. Feeling her way like a blind person, Abbie soon discovered that she was at the bottom of the staircase and her eyes began to adjust to the darkness. There were a few small windows that were level with the ground outside which allowed small amounts of light to pierce the darkness.

Abbie got her bearings and inched her way towards the area where the vault should be. Her small flashlight gave just enough light to lead the way. Just as she thought, there were concrete walls outlining a space that was the same as the vault above. Abbie started on one side of the square formation and felt the walls, looking for an entrance.

There was nothing on the first three sides she investigated. Nothing but old boxes and junk piled up against the walls. When Abbie turned the next corner, she could see more piles of junk, but these were stacked up at least six or seven feet high. They almost reached the ceiling. It looked as if someone was trying to hide something.

A feeling in the pit of her stomach told her that she was on to something. Abbie placed the small key ring flashlight between her teeth so she could use both hands. Working quickly, she started pulling things away from the wall. Some of the boxes were heavy, very heavy and it was all that Abbie could do to lift them out of the way.

After moving one of the heaviest boxes, her eyes caught a glimpse of wood in the wall, not concrete. Abbie worked faster. She used every last bit of strength she had to move the remaining boxes. She couldn't believe her eyes. There, in front of her, was a small wooden door. It was not much bigger than the hatch that led to her secret underground office. As she inspected the edges around the door, she realized that at one time the door had been covered up with concrete. From the looks of it, someone had chiseled away the concrete to expose the door once again.

Abbie pulled on the small door and it swung open easily. She shined her flashlight into the hole, where she saw the all too familiar signs of the tunnel system. Abbie reached into her pocket and took out her cell phone. She knew that once she entered the tunnels, there wouldn't be a signal strong enough to transmit. Abbie called Jane at the police station, but only got her voice mail. She left her a message and then stuffed the phone back into her pocket. Well, here goes nothing. Abbie thought to herself as she took a deep breath and crawled into the darkness.

Chapter Twenty-Four

The space was just like the tunnel entrance at the old Robinson house. It wasn't too big and the walls were dirt and it smelled musty and old. Abbie wiped the sweat from her brow and shined her flashlight around the room. To her left, she saw where the wall stopped and the tunnel obviously continued to connect with the other tunnels. As she stepped towards the opening she realized that her shoes squished as she walked. She deduced that when the water in the river rose, it caused water to be pushed into the tunnels. This is why Walter Carson's skull eventually worked its way out of the tunnel system and into the creek at Crybaby Hollow.

Abbie had only taken a few steps into the tunnel, when the small beam of her flashlight reflected off of something ahead. With her feet sloshing in the dampness, she moved closer to the sparkles. She didn't need a large flashlight to realize what she had found. There, resting on a stone slab was a large pile of gold bricks.

Abbie picked up one of the bricks, which was very heavy, and examined it with her flashlight. She took a deep breath and looked skyward, "Thank you!"

"You're welcome," a voice said from behind.

Chapter Twenty-Five

Abbie quickly turned around to find Ray Strickland standing in the tunnel holding a gun - and pointing it at her. Abbie gasped and dropped the gold brick, which barely missed her foot.

"Careful," he said quietly. "Why don't you come with me?"

Abbie had no choice. She slowly moved towards Mr. Strickland, who started backing out of the tunnel. Abbie kept her eyes on the gun. It wasn't the first time a gun had been pointed at her, but that didn't make it any less terrifying.

Mr. Strickland crawled out of the small opening into the basement. Abbie followed, trying not to make any sudden moves that would make him nervous. He walked over to a switch box and flipped on the breaker, which turned on a string of light bulbs that illuminated the basement. Mr. Strickland took a chair from the piles of furniture in one corner and placed it in front of Abbie.

Chapter Twenty-Five

"Have a seat," he ordered.

Abbie sat down in the seat, never taking her eyes off of Mr. Strickland.

"So, super-sleuth, how did you figure it out?" he asked. "What gave me away?"

Abbie took a breath. Should she tell him what she knew? Did she really have it all figured out? Perhaps, she could get him to tell her more and fill in the gaps. "Well, it was the research paper you gave me. The dates didn't match up."

"Well, aren't you the smart one," he said smugly.

"Of course, I didn't really know for sure until I found the letter that Stephen Dalton wrote to James...James Adams, who served in the Confederate Army with your great-grand-father, John Strickland."

Ray Strickland's eyes opened wider with astonishment. "What letter? Where did you find–"

Before she realized it, she was interrupting him. "In the old trunk that had the Confederate money. You remember the one...the one that my friend and I found and you planted?" Ray Strickland's eyebrows raised in disbelief. "There is no way that trunk of money sat down there in those tunnels for over a hundred years. You see, what you didn't count on was the river."

"The river? What do you mean the river?" he quizzed.

"When the river rises, the tunnels flood. If the trunk had been down there, the trunk would have been rusted on the bottom and it wasn't. It wasn't even that dirty on the bottom. I am guessing that you planted the trunk down there right after Tyler and I found the skull. You knew that people would be searching for the rest of Walter Carson and if they found the trunk full of money, then all of the 'gold chasers' as you call them, would stop searching for the gold."

"I am very, very impressed," Ray Strickland said.

"The dates of your report didn't match the dates that Stephen Dalton put in his letter. I guess you never found the false bottom of the trunk?"

"No," Ray Strickland began. "My great-grandfather had one last conversation with Stephen Dalton before he died. He told him where the payroll and the gold were stashed. I suppose he forget to tell him about the letter. James Adams and my grandfather were mortally wounded on the battlefield shortly after that but my great-grandfather managed to get off one last letter to my great-grandmother before he died. When I was doing research twenty years ago, I found the letter in an old wardrobe that belonged to her."

"And, I am assuming that with the help of Walter Carson, you found it," Abbie added.

"You don't miss a thing, do you?" he smirked.

"Walter Carson was a history professor at the University of Virginia, who specialized in the Civil War and buildings of the 1800's. Did he get in your way? Did you get greedy?"

"Yes!" Ray Strickland admitted. "If you want to know the truth, yes! He got in the way - wanted to turn the gold into the state and...well, I just couldn't let him do that, now could I?"

"So you killed him!" Abbie shouted.

"Yes," he said coldly. "I took care of old Walter."

"Did you know that he also worked for the government?" Abbie asked.

"No," Ray Strickland admitted. "It wasn't until the men in the dark suits started poking around asking questions, that I got really nervous. So, I told them that he came here, met with me and then got on a bus and that was the last I heard of him." He paced back and forth, rubbing his temples. Then he spoke in an aggravated voice, "Then you and your friends spoiled everything! I could have kept living off of this gold for the rest of my life, but now I have to figure out what to do with you. You know too much!"

Before the last word could exit his mouth, Abbie heard the click of a gun being cocked. "Hold it!" She turned toward the sound. It was Jane Galloway. "Freeze! Put the gun on the ground and put your hands on your head. Do it!" Ray Strickland complied. "Now, get down on your hands and knees and lay face down on the floor!"

Ray Strickland did so and as soon as he was flat on the floor, Abbie moved quickly over to Jane on the stairs. She hugged her tightly and for the first time in the past ten minutes breathed easily.

Jane motioned for the police officers behind her to move in and take Ray Strickland into custody. She led Abbie up to the main lobby while the other officers read Ray Strickland his rights and hauled him out to the police car.

When Jane realized that Abbie had stopped shaking, she pushed the hair out of her face and looked her in the eye. "It's a good thing I check my voice mail? Do me a favor. Don't do anything this stupid again!"

Abbie only smiled and hugged her. She couldn't make any promises.

Chapter Twenty-Six

December 24th

They say it ain't over until it's over. Finally, the mystery of the gold, the skull and dear old Walter Carson has come to an end. Of course, I may be grounded from now until my 18th birthday for doing what I did, but oh well...it was very exciting. It's been about a week now since my encounter with Ray Strickland, and I'm happy to say he is on his way to the slammer, probably for life. The gold is in the hands of the city council, which will probably end up getting taken by the state, but all of that is out of my hands. I'm just glad that it's over. Dianne now knows that her father was right. There was gold in them there hills! or tunnels in this case. Kirk was quite jealous of my last underground adventure. But he felt like he had a big part in it anyway. It was his research on the Confederate Army that helped me put it all together when I found that letter. All those weeks after we found Kirk and Brian, I just knew there was something missing...something that just didn't make the puzzle complete. The hidden letter was the last clue that made everything make sense.

I emailed Becca, though I was supposed to be grounded from the computer and basically "life" in general. However, Dad let me shoot off one email to Memphis. She was excited about what happened. She said she wished she had been here to use her karate on Ray Strickland. And believe it or not, I finally broke down and told her about bringing Sarah into the agency. She wasn't mad! I was shocked! She like totally understood. I'm glad. Sarah is going to be quite useful. And anyway, four heads are better than two.

Becca said she wants to come here for spring break. I am so excited! Even though we are not as close as we used to be, I miss her all the time...and you know, I think she misses me too. So, I'm looking forward to spring break.

It's Christmas Eve and I'm getting ready to go to bed, if I can go to sleep. I feel like I'm six years old again! It's the hardest night in the whole year to fall asleep. At least when I do fall asleep, I won't have to worry about having the nightmare. Which, this brings me to my latest dilemma.

This afternoon when I got home from Christmas shopping, I found a package on my bed. Dad signed for it, and thank heavens he didn't open it. The return address is simply NSO, with Natty's name on it. I haven't opened it yet. Natty said she would be in touch and I REALLY want to open it...but I'm kind of scared to, knowing what I know.

Maybe I'll open it tomorrow...